SHE KNELT BEFORE THE OPEN TRUNK

A LITTLE MAID

OF

NEWPORT

By
ALICE TURNER CURTIS

Author of
"The Little Maid Historical Books"
"Yankee Girl Civil War Stories"

Illustrated by
Hattie Longstreet Price

APPLEWOOD BOOKS
Bedford, Massachusetts

A Little Maid of Newport was first published by
the Penn Publishing Company in 1935.

Thank you for purchasing an Applewood
book. Applewood reprints America's lively
classics—books from the past that are still of
interest to modern readers. For a free copy of
our current catalog, write to:

Applewood Books
P.O. Box 365
Bedford, MA 01730

ISBN 1-55709-339-3

Printed and bound in Canada.

10 9 8 7 6 5 4 3 2 1

Contents

Illustrations

A Little Maid of Newport

CHAPTER I

SURPRISES

"ONLY two days to Ellen's birthday," Faith
Underwood reminded herself, as she opened the
narrow attic window and looked out over the field
which sloped down to the harbor of Newport, Rhode
Island, where now, in March 1777, she could see the
ships of the British fleet.

"I wish I could give her a real present, like a workbox
with a thimble and scissors," she thought, remembering her cousin's admiration of the silk-lined box of
polished wood fitted with cases of needles, threads of
various colors, a silver thimble, and scissors of different sizes that they had seen in the shop of Mistress
Ware. But, with a little sigh, Faith gave up the thought
of bestowing such a gift, and again peered out of the
window.

"There goes Mark," she whispered as she saw a tall
boy hurrying down the lane which led toward the
town. And, with another quick glance toward the
harbor, Faith closed the window against the chill

March wind, tied her blue quilted hood over her neatly braided yellow hair, and taking up the cape of blue flannel from the chair near the window she ran across the room, opened the door and went softly down the steep stairway. Although she moved as quietly as possible her stout leather shoes made an echoing thud that Faith feared surely would bring her aunt to the front hallway.

"And she would tell me 'tis too cold to go wandering along the shore, just as she did yesterday," thought Faith as she reached the top of the wide stairway that led to the lower hall. Smiling with satisfaction Faith gazed at the polished bannisters, and in an instant, as swiftly and noiselessly as a bird in flight, she was sliding down their shining surface and, with a little chuckle of delight, she opened the front door and ran down the slope.

"Ellen won't be back from her errand for a good half-hour. If Aunt Cynthia misses me she will think I am with Ellen," Faith told herself as she hurried on, her thoughts full of the surprise she was planning for her cousin's birthday.

She kept close to a thick growth of young spruce trees that bordered one side of the field so that she could not be seen from the windows of her Uncle Morley's house, that since the death of her father and mother two years earlier had been her home, and quickly reached the cove whose sandy beach was a favorite playground of the two girls. Here Mark, Ellen's elder brother, a boy of fourteen, sometimes joined them to show his skill in "skipping" small flat stones over the quiet waters of the cove, or with a long pole vaulting from the beach to some high point of the rocky ledge which ran out into the harbor.

But this morning, a sunny March day of 1777, Faith had it all to herself save for a flock of noisy gulls that hovered over the ledge. As she ran along the beach she sent a resentful glance toward the British warships that now lay at anchor in the harbor. This fleet, which to the consternation of the people of Newport, Rhode Island, had, in December 1776, landed eight thousand English soldiers, under the command of General Clinton and Earl Percy, and which now, to the menace of the safety and comfort of loyal American residents, controlled the town.

"They are just like those old pirates Uncle Morley told me about," thought Faith, recalling her uncle's stories of the early days of the town when pirate ships had infested this coast, capturing vessels laden with rich cargoes, sinking fishing boats, and raiding the settlements. They hid their plunder in caves along the shore until they were taken prisoners and paid the penalty of their crimes on "Gallows Field," near the Powder-house at Newport.

"I wonder how long before they'll fire on the town, as Mark says they surely will," Faith thought fearfully.

For the British soldiers had already burned many houses, cut down orchards for fuel, and dismantled churches, as well as plundering the homes of such citizens as resisted their authority; and Faith knew that her uncle and aunt kept a sharp outlook to the safety of their own homes, and that Mark took every care to conceal his boat for fear some wandering soldier might take possession of it. So it was small wonder that the little girl looked upon the British fleet with dread.

"I would well like to cut all their anchor chains and see those ships drift straight onto the rocks. I wonder why Newport men don't go out in boats some night and do that," thought Faith, unaware of the sharp watch constantly kept night and day against any possible attack by the Americans who were resolved that England's unjust rule over the American Colonies should end. Already Washington's Army had driven the British from Boston, and American ships were now capturing many English vessels loaded with supplies. But New York was an English stronghold, and now Newport, which for so many years had outrivaled New York and Boston in its prosperity, in the number of ships that sailed from its port, and in the elegance of its established homes, was apparently at the mercy of the British feet.

But Faith's blue eyes shone with a new purpose as she told herself that there was surely some way to send the threatening ships adrift; and as she climbed the rough ledge she imagined herself setting forth in Mark's boat to accomplish the deed that might free Newport from the menace of the British fleet.

"I'd best be thinking of Ellen's birthday," she reminded herself as she reached the highest point of the ledge and crept cautiously among the rocks to a narrow opening that led to a small cave, which Faith earnestly believed was known to no one save herself.

The entrance to this deep cavity was nearly hidden by a small scrubby oak tree, whose rough branches she now pushed aside and carefully lowered herself to the rough floor of the cave, several feet below the opening. From an unlucky tumble on her discovery of this cave Faith had learned the danger of missing her foothold; but she was now able to slide easily down to the shadowy chamber.

"'Tis just like being in the woods," she whispered, looking about with smiling satisfaction, and forgetting all about the British ships as she gazed admiringly at the branches of fir and spruce with which the rough walls were nearly covered. For over a week Faith had worked industriously bringing armfuls of these branches and fastening them over the rocky sides of the cave. As she had done this secretly, at such times as she was sure her cousins would not wonder as to her whereabouts, it had meant hard work.

But now, although Faith's preparations were not

yet complete for Ellen's birthday surprise, the little girl was well pleased by what she had already accomplished.

"Only two more days," she thought happily, "and Ellen will be twelve years old, just my age; and even if I can't give her a real present, like a workbox or a locket, I can give her this cave. We can have it for our secret place," and Faith now set happily to work covering a pile of dry seaweed with fir boughs.

"That makes a fine seat, and if I only had some sort of a table," she thought, wondering if she could possibly discover anything that would serve as a table.

But a noise, as of someone climbing the ledge just below the entrance to the cave, made her spring to her feet fearful that someone besides herself had discovered it and was about to enter. Then the sound of voices, and in a moment Faith realized that two men had seated themselves near the scrubby oak tree, had lighted their pipes and evidently settled down to enjoy the sunshine and the view over the harbor.

"If I make the least noise they will surely hear and begin to search," she thought; for the newcomers were so near that she knew she could easily reach out through the opening and touch them; and when they again began talking Faith gave a little gasp of terror. "They are British sailors," she told herself, and now listened intently as the men began speaking of an old vessel, the *Beach Bird*, which had lain for years dismantled at one of the wharves, and which the British had taken possession of, and were now converting into an armed galley to aid them in conquering the Americans.

"The old craft has a strange history," one of the men declared, "and I'd not like to sail in her. 'Tis said in 1750, or thereabouts, this vessel came sailing in close to shore with all sails set, and grounded on the beach. Some fishermen boarded her, but there was not a soul on board. But there was a kettle boiling over the galley fire, the table set for breakfast, a dog in the cabin, and everything in order. The fellow who told me the tale said that's all they ever knew about the craft—never knew what became of the crew."

"I like not what I hear of this coast," responded the other in a surly voice. "Too many tales of pirates captured and hung, and of caves along these ledges, where like as not these rebel Americans can hide their arms and plan to attack our fleet."

"I mean to make a search for those caves. This ledge would be a likely place, and maybe I'd have luck and find some well hidden treasure," came the answer; and hearing this Faith wondered what would happen next.

"If they push aside the branches of the oak tree they'll surely see the opening," she thought fearfully; "they'll get a tumble anyway," and the little girl gave a convulsive giggle as she imagined the men falling head first down the entrance. Then she knew they had risen to their feet and were moving off.

For a few moments Faith kept perfectly still. Not until the last sound of their retreating feet had died away did she venture to move, and then, without even a glance behind her, she climbed up to the surface of the ledge, peered cautiously between the branches of the oak tree, and hurried off toward home.

"Those old Britishers spoil everything," she thought unhappily. "That man saying he was going to search for caves might come just when Ellen and I were there," and Faith raced along the smooth beach; but a familiar call, a loud clear whistle three times repeated, made her stop suddenly and a moment later she saw Ellen running toward her.

"Wherever have you been, Faith! Mother was sure you were busy with your patchwork, and I searched the house through for you! Oh, you can never guess what's happened," and, without waiting for any response, Ellen seized Faith by the arm and exclaimed: "Letty Stevens is going to have a birthday party for me! Isn't that fine!" and Ellen danced about her cousin too excited to notice Faith's unhappy expression.

The two girls were about the same height and complexion, and were usually dressed alike, so they were sometimes mistaken for each other. But while Ellen was always easily amused Faith was more serious. To Ellen the British fleet, and the red-coated English soldiers who took possession of whatever house they pleased, seemed of no great importance; while to Ellen's brother, Mark, and to Faith, they seemed a constant menace, and Faith was always wondering if there might not be some way in which she could help the loyal Americans to free themselves from these unwelcome visitors.

Talking happily of the party Ellen did not quickly notice her cousin's silence.

"Letty says it's going to be a different kind of a party; that we'll all be surprised. She is going to invite Wealthy Richards, and Mary Clement and Lucy and Jane Atwater. Maybe Mother will let us wear our silk dresses. Why, Faith! You haven't said a word!" Ellen at last exclaimed. "Don't you think it will be fun?"

"The Atwater girls are Tories. Uncle Morley said so," Faith declared.

"No matter! Two Tory girls don't count," laughed Ellen, "and the Stevens' house is lovely for a party. Letty has a music-box and everything. Oh, Faith, what do you suppose the surprise is?"

But poor Faith, thinking of the defeat of her own surprise for Ellen's birthday, could find little to say; and she walked on beside her cousin wondering if the sailors who had sat near the cave's entrance that morning would discover the opening and be surprised to find it so well prepared for visitors.

As the girls climbed the slope Ellen exclaimed: "I

almost forgot about tomorrow! Oh, all sorts of things are happening this week! Mother says we can go fishing with Mark tomorrow, and take our lunch. We'll build a fire on the ledges and cook a fish and bake potatoes."

"Truly, Ellen?" Faith eagerly responded, her face brightening. For a fishing excursion with Mark meant that they would have a day of wandering along the shore to the ledges that ran out into the harbor, from whose rocks they would fish for bass and tautogs, and at noonday feast happily in some sheltered cove.

"Hallie will bake us a corncake to take with us," continued Ellen, "and we'll be sure to find May flowers along the edge of the woods above the shore. We'll wear our old shoes and skirts. Whatever made you wear a hood today, Faith? March is half over."

"I don't know why I put it on," said Faith, untying the ribbons of her hood and pulling it off. "Let's go to the kitchen and tell Hallie to be sure the corncake is crispy. I don't like the crumby kind; do you, Ellen?"

"Come on," agreed Ellen, and the cousins ran across the yard to the rear of the house and pushed open the door of the big kitchen, where Hallie, the negro servant, was preparing the midday meal.

Hallie usually welcomed the girls to her kitchen with wide smiles, bobbing her turbaned head and offering them a taste of any special dish that she was cooking. But this morning she made no response to their greeting, and muttered to herself as Ellen began to tell her of the proposed excursion and to ask if the corncake might not be: "All crispy, Hallie. You know the kind we like, the kind that crackles when we break it."

As Ellen finished the big negro woman turned and faced her visitors with such evident alarm in her expression that the girls gazed at her in silent amazement.

"You telling me your folks letting you go a-scrumaging off into danger that way! Ain't dis place infested with pirates in red coats taking every last thing there is? I ain't gwine ter make no corncake fer such doings. 'Twould be snatched right out of your hands if those sojers happened to see it," declared Hallie.

"But, Hallie, the British are in the forts, or on the ships, or in the town. We'll be going straight away from them, out on the ledges. We'll bring home a nice catch of bass and tautogs," pleaded Faith.

"You'll fall to your death from those slippery ledges, dat is if de redcoats don't push you off and take Master Mark prisoner. I ain't gwine ter make no corncake for you. And don't you be blaming me, Missy Ellen, if you don't have a birthday cake. I got no sugar, no raisins, no spice, nothing; all on account of these Tory soldiers overrunning de place," and Hallie turned back to her work; and Ellen and Faith, exchanging a look of understanding, made their way through the kitchen, crossed a small hallway, and entered a pleasant room that faced toward Newport harbor.

Not until they had closed the door behind them did they venture to speak, then they both exclaimed: "Hallie's upset because she can't make a birthday cake!"

"She will make the corncake just the same, see if she doesn't," Ellen added, for Hallie had never yet failed to do her best for the family she had faithfully served since she was a young girl when, in a slave ship from Africa, she had first seen her future home. For the time between 1750 and 1760 Newport was the great slave mart for America; and the foundation of many great fortunes of Newport citizens was based on this trade.

When Hallie was in good humor Mark and the girls well liked to linger in the big kitchen and listen to her stories of far-off Africa; of the dreadful weeks of her voyage to America. Nor did Hallie ever fail to end her tales by telling of the kindness of "Ole Miss," Ellen's grandmother, who had purchased the young slave girl, treated her kindly and taught her to become a good cook.

That afternoon Faith had little time to recall her visit to the cave, for Aunt Cynthia reminded the girls that they were to recite their lessons to her directly after dinner.

"As you will be away tomorrow we will have an extra hour of study today," Mrs. Morley smilingly declared, as if confident this extra hour was exactly what the girls were hoping for.

"You can use part of that time practicing your hand-writing, for I am sorry to say I find little improvement in it," she added, as Ellen and Faith followed her into the living-room and seated themselves beside a low narrow table which stood between the two windows facing the harbor.

When, with the arrival of the British soldiers, the schools of Newport had been obliged to close Mrs. Morley had at once decided on regular hours of study and recitation for Mark and the girls. But Mark's hours came at a different time from those of Ellen's and Faith's, as his father was his instructor.

At first the girls had been well pleased with the plan, declaring it was not a bit like school, and thinking it an easy matter to learn to repeat poems, to recite the facts of the early history of Rhode Island, to draw maps of New England, and to figure how much a dress would cost if its material was priced at a shilling a yard and you bought seven and one-third yards.

But as the days grew warmer they began to find it more difficult to stay quietly indoors; and today Ellen's thoughts were centered not only on the fishing excursion but on the birthday party with its promised surprise; while Faith found it no easy matter not to recall the talk of the two British sailors, and to wonder if they might not find the entrance to the cave before she again visited it.

"And I haven't any present for Ellen," she thought unhappily, remembering the pair of fine white stockings that her cousin had knitted for her as a birthday gift.

But before the afternoon ended Faith's spirits brightened; she had decided what she would give Ellen. It was one of her own dearest possessions, something that she knew her cousin would well like to possess.

CHAPTER II

MARK was ready and waiting for the two girls when they opened the kitchen door the next morning. With his high leather boots, into which were tucked his trousers of brown homespun, and wearing a short oilskin jacket over his blue flannel shirt, he looked ready for any emergency.

"Oh, pirate's cap!" exclaimed Ellen, glancing smilingly at the square of bright blue cotton that Mark had twisted about his head, tying it in a double knot above his forehead in the same way favored by the old sailors whom he saw about the wharves.

He carried a covered basket containing the potatoes they would cook for their midday meal, and the crisp corncake, carefully wrapped, which Hallie had handed him with a muttered word of warning not to let the "redcoat pirates" get hold of it; and she now followed the girls from the kitchen repeating her warnings of the dangers she felt sure they would encounter. Not until they were out of sight did the big negro woman, shaking her turbaned head over the perils of such an excursion, return to her work.

The Morley house lay well beyond the town, and

21

the family had so far escaped any serious annoyance from the enemy's troops; and now as Ellen and Faith followed Mark along the narrow path that circled a thick growth of tall pine trees they had little fear of encountering any danger. Their way led them to the brow of a hill, and here they stopped for a brief rest and to look out over the harbor where the British war vessels lay at anchor, and where boats were coming and going between the ships and the wharves of the town.

Toward the north lay many small islands, one of which, called Coaster's Harbor, was known to them as the place where John Clarke, with his little band of followers, had landed in 1639, searching for a place to found a settlement.

But they were all too eager to get to the ledges, which lay beyond the rough pasture land, to linger long on the hilltop; and Faith ran down the slope bidding her companions to hurry, and Mark quickly overtook her. Ellen, however, sauntered along singing:

> "'Twas in the reign of George the Third,
>   Our public peace was much disturb'd
>   By ships of war that came and laid
>   Within our ports to stop our trade.
>   Which does provoke to high degree
>   Our true-born Sons of Liberty,
>   So that 'tis hard for them to bear
>   The sight of warships lying there."

"Lucky we are not within hearing of English soldiers," said Mark as he and Faith waited for Ellen to catch up with them.

"You'd best not be quite so ready with your songs, Ellen," he warned her as she joined them.

"You are as bad as Hallie," Ellen laughingly responded. "She is sure there's a redcoat behind every bush ready to grab us. Maybe they would take us on board one of the warships and we would see Earl Percy and Brigadier-General Richard Prescott," and Ellen skipped along as if a sight of these high officers of the English forces would well repay her for being taken captive.

"I can see General Prescott easily enough; his headquarters are in the Bannister house, right across from the Congregational Church. You could see him any pleasant day strolling about, and if any boy or man dares pass him without taking off his hat the general has him arrested as a rebel," said Mark; "but we boys manage to turn before we meet him," he added with evident satisfaction in being able to avoid tribute to the vain and arrogant English officer who was heartily disliked even by his own soldiers.

They were now well beyond sight of their own home and the outlying farms, and could hear the roar of the surf as the breakers dashed against the dangerous rocks of Brenton's Reef, which extended a mile into the sea.

"We'll get a good catch today," declared Mark, as they made their way to the shore; and, cautioned by Mark to take no chances of slipping, the girls followed him along the rocky ledges until they reached a small hollow between the rocks where they were sheltered from the sea wind.

"We'll leave our basket here," Mark decided; "'tis a fine place to build a fire, and we can come here with our fish."

The girls promptly agreed; for it was well understood that on these excursions Mark was the leader, and as he was responsible for their safety and thoughtful for their comfort neither Ellen nor Faith questioned his decisions, and they at once looked about them for the best place to start a fire.

"Right here in this sandy place," said Ellen. "Faith and I will fetch driftwood and sticks and have it all ready for you to light, Mark, when you bring a fish;" for neither of the girls cared much about the real fishing, and Mark picked up the canvas bag that held his hooks and lines, and the bait he had made ready at home, and, again cautioning them to keep near this sheltered cove, Mark made ready to start off for the point where he had decided to fish.

"I'll leave my flint and steel so you can start the fire. See, I'll put the box on top of the basket," he told them, and the girls promised that he should find a good bed of hot coals ready to broil the fish and roast the potatoes on his return; and they at once began their search for clusters of dry seaweed, bits of wood and sticks that the tides had washed up along the shore.

"I'll go this way, Ellen, and you go the other," said Faith, after they had carefully placed the basket on a little shelf of rock, "and if you want me just whistle." For the three long whistles were always their signal to attract each other's attention; and, agreeing that Faith should be the one to secure seaweed while Ellen would search for wood, the girls started off.

Climbing cautiously among the rocks Faith had soon gathered an armful, and was about to start back to the little cove when a queer noise made her stop suddenly, and look anxiously in the direction of the sound.

"Maybe some bird is caught in those rocks," she thought, peering up along the rough reef. "I'll climb up and find out;" and, depositing her seaweed in a safe nook between the rocks, Faith cautiously started up the ledge pausing now and then to listen, and from time to time again hearing the low moan as of some creature in pain.

"It's more like a child than a bird," she told herself, as she came steadily nearer the place from which it was evident the sound came.

No thought of fear had entered her mind, so that as she peered around a mass of rocks and suddenly beheld a man lying there she gave a quick exclamation that made him gaze at her in wondering surprise.

"What is the matter?" she demanded, too surprised to think of fear, and quickly noticing his thin face, and that his clothing was ragged and torn. "Did you fall from the ledge?" she added, going toward him and wishing Mark was there.

The man nodded, moving his head from side to side, as if too weak to speak; but as Faith bent over him he whispered: "Two days."

"Oh! Do you mean 'tis two days you have been here?" and he nodded again.

"I'll help you," the little girl promptly declared. "I'll be right back," she added, and was off before he could even nod in response, and she was off down the ledge regardless that her haste might send her tumbling to the shore, and was quickly back at the sheltered cove.

Seizing the basket, and thrusting the metal box that held the flint and steel into the deep pocket of her skirt, Faith turned back and, breathless and fearful for the safety of the helpless man, again climbed the ledge and found that he had managed to raise himself to a sitting posture, his back resting against the ledge.

Without a word Faith opened the basket, drew out the jug filled with milk and carried it to him; but he was too weak to hold it, and the little girl steadied it carefully so that he could drink. Then breaking bits from the corn bread she fed the nearly famished man, whose dark eyes gave her a glance of gratitude; and by the time he had devoured the last bit of the corncake and finished the milk he was able to speak.

But his story came haltingly, for he was exhausted by days without food, and by the unlucky fall that had sent him tumbling among the rocks to lie bruised and suffering, too weak to make further effort.

"You won't tell anyone where I am?" he earnestly pleaded. "You mustn't do that. I am a deserter from the British Army. They'll be searching for me, but if I can manage to get a bit more strength I'll get away."

"My cousin Mark would help you, I know he would," Faith earnestly responded, but the man shook his head, repeating his demand that she should promise never to tell of her discovery, and this Faith reluctantly agreed to.

"But your shoes are all worn out, and you haven't any hat, and how can you get away when you can't stand up?" she questioned, taking off her warm flannel cape and wrapping it about his thin shoulders as he shivered in the sharp wind from the sea; and without waiting for his reply she quickly added:

"I'll bring you some things, and food too. And I promise not to tell anyone about you. I'll start a fire now and roast these potatoes."

"A sure way to bring someone after me. No fire! Why 'tis just what the soldiers would be looking for. But I'd well like the potatoes," he responded. "I am hungrier than ever after my taste of milk and corn bread."

"The jug holds a quart and you drank it all, and 'twas a good sized corncake," she reminded him, and he nodded smilingly.

"A feast, and as much as I should eat," he declared; and Faith, now looking about the rocky ledge where the suffering man must stay until he regained enough strength to make a further effort to escape, began to wonder how she could do something to add a bit of comfort to his refuge.

"I know what I'll do," she exclaimed. "I'll bring up the dry seaweed and make you a bed," and she was off before he could reply.

By the time she had carried several armfuls of dry seaweed up the steep ledge Faith was almost too tired to heap it up so that the man could manage to move himself toward it. But she resolutely persisted, and felt herself rewarded when he said that it was the easiest bed a soldier need wish for. "There isn't any fresh water nearby, is there?" he asked, as Faith spread her cape over him saying that she must go.

"I know of a spring! I'll fill the jug and bring it back. And early tomorrow morning I'll come again," she promised.

The spring Faith had spoken of was well known to the Morley children on account of their frequent excursions to the ledges. It bubbled up in the sand where the pastureland sloped down to the shore near the little cove, where they had planned to eat their noonday meal.

"I mustn't let Ellen see me," thought the tired girl as she made her way toward it, for Ellen's shrill whistle now echoed among the rocks. With great caution Faith managed to reach the spring and fill the jug without being discovered, and carried it back to the wanderer, who falteringly told her something of his gratitude as she bade him good-bye.

"Oh, dear! I don't know what Mark will do when he finds the basket gone," thought Faith, as at the foot of the ledge she at last sent a response to Ellen's whistle, and in a few moments saw her cousins hurrying to meet her; before they reached her Ellen called:

"'Tis just as Hallie said. Those soldiers have taken our corncake!"

"What soldiers? Where are they?" Faith responded in such evident terror that Mark promptly declared:

"On their way back to the fort," and as they now turned back together he continued:

"There were two of them, hunting for a runaway. They came out where I was fishing and questioned me if I had seen any trace of the fellow. They thought he might be hiding among the rocks. If I had seen him I wouldn't have told them. I'd help him get away. I wonder you didn't see the redcoats, Faith."

"Oh, Mark! Are you sure they are gone?" said Faith, clutching at her cousin's arm, and looking wildly about.

"Don't be frightened, Faith. They are surely back at the fort by this time. I watched them as they left the ledges and started off across the pasture," Mark assured her.

"And they took our basket, and Mark's tinderbox, and your cape, Faith," declared Ellen, noticing that her cousin's cape was missing.

"We might as well start for home; we have nothing to eat, and I have two good-sized bass to take along," said Mark.

But Faith pleaded for a little rest before they started; and as they were near the bubbling spring she knelt down and drank thirstily, and they seated themselves on the sandy beach.

Ellen and Mark were both too excited over Mark's encounter with the soldiers to notice how tired their cousin looked, and Faith could think only of how nearly the deserter had come to being captured.

"What would they do to the man if they did find him?" she asked.

"They said General Prescott would hang him, as a warning to other soldiers. There are lots of redcoats who would run off if they dared," Mark replied.

"Come on, let's start for home. 'Tis well past noon, and I never was so hungry," declared Ellen, and Mark was eager to be off, so Faith plodded wearily along after them, her thoughts busy with plans for aiding the helpless man who might so easily be discovered and punished for his effort to escape.

Mrs. Morley and Hallie listened to Mark's story of their morning's adventure, and his mother promptly announced that there were to be no more such excursions.

"You children must promise me to keep more closely at home. Now that Sir Henry Clinton has left Newport, and Earl Percy is in command of the English forces here, General Prescott has more power than ever; and he does not care what his soldiers do to make life difficult for American patriots. All we can do is to keep away from them. Why, Faith, you look tired out, and no wonder; Hallie will give you your dinner as soon as she can, and then you girls had best lie down and rest."

"I'm not tired," responded Ellen; but as soon as she had finished her dinner Faith was quite ready to go to her room and rest.

Slipping off the worn flannel dress and her heavy shoes, she put on the quilted wrapper that had been her aunt's Christmas gift to her, turned back the white tufted bedspread, and lay thankfully down on the neat bed.

But she had too much to think about to sleep. She must in some way secure clothing and food and carry it to the unprotected man who had trusted to her help. As for the clothing, she had already decided about that. Stored in the Morley attic were various possessions that had belonged to Faith's parents. Among these was a trunk containing her father's clothing.

"Aunt Cynthia said the things were all mine; and that when the right time came I could decide what to do with them, and this is the right time," Faith told herself.

The house was now very quiet. Mark had gone on an errand to the town; Ellen was happily visiting with Hallie in the kitchen, and Faith knew that her aunt was busy with her sewing.

"If I go to the attic now no one will know it," she thought, forgetting her fatigue in her eagerness to make sure of the clothing, and in a few moments she was kneeling before the open trunk.

"Shirts!" she whispered, lifting out a pile of white linen garments, and then a bag containing stockings.

"I'll take one shirt, and two pairs of stockings, and a coat and these grey trousers," she decided, and was carefully closing the trunk when she remembered the man's shoes that were too worn to protect his feet, and again explored among the carefully packed contents, but failed to discover any sort of slipper or boot.

With a little sigh of disappointment Faith gathered up the garments, rolling the coat, trousers, shirt and stockings into as compact a bundle as possible, and tying them together with a strong cord. Then, carrying the package, she returned to her room. Pushing it well under the bed she again stretched herself out to rest, and was fast asleep until Ellen came to tell her that supper was ready.

CHAPTER III

THE PARTY

FAITH slept but little that night. She planned to creep out of the house before anyone was awake the next morning, and long before daylight she slipped noiselessly from the bed without awakening Ellen, dressed as quickly as possible, and carrying the package of clothing made her way to the kitchen.

Resting the bundle on one of the kitchen chairs the little girl opened the pantry door and looked anxiously about.

"I'll take what's left of the chicken, and those russet apples," she decided, thrusting the food into a basket which stood on a nearby shelf, and adding eggs from the big wooden bowl, and a square of gingerbread from the stone jar.

Hurrying back to the kitchen her glance happened to light on Mark's stout leather shoes standing under a bench, and these she promptly tied to her bundle of clothing.

"Mark's feet are as large as Uncle Morley's; maybe the man can wear them. If he can't I'll bring them back," she thought, and now, ready for the long walk, Faith opened the outer door and stepped out.

There was only a glimmer of dawn along the eastern horizon. The big elm in the yard cast its dark shadow toward the house, and a chilly wind made her glad of her woolen jacket and of the knit cap that she had pulled over her yellow braids.

Burdened with the package and basket Faith hurried off along the familiar path, and by the time the sun was well up she was at the foot of the ledge. Leaving the clothing, she grasped the handle of the basket and began to climb up the rocky height. Early as she was the man was awake.

"You really mean to help me," he said, as if he could hardly credit such a thing; and when Faith opened the basket and bade him help himself the poor fellow peered into it with an exclamation of delight.

"I'll fill the jug now, and then I'll fetch the clothes," said Faith, "and maybe when I come tomorrow you'll be strong enough to start for a cave I know about, where you can hide 'til you can plan what to do," and before he could make any response she was off, and quickly returned with the fresh water.

At the sight of the decent clothing the man's face brightened, and when he found Mark's shoes a comfortable fit he declared himself able to start off at once. But it was evident that he still had but little strength.

"It's going to be warmer, and after you put on these things you'll feel better," Faith assured him. "You must lie quiet and rest all you can until I come for you. My name is Faith Underwood," she added, "and I live with my Uncle Philip Morley."

The man repeated her name thoughtfully, and said:

"My first friend in this new land. And be sure I'll never forget your name, little maid. My name is Hugh Ramsay," he added.

"That's a fine name. Earl Percy's name is Hugh, and people say he likes not to fight against us. Now I'll hurry home before they miss me. I'll come for you tomorrow," and with a smiling nod Faith bade him good-bye.

She made the return journey very quickly, and her only anxiety was to get into the house without being discovered. It was now broad daylight, and she knew Hallie was sure to be up, and that her uncle and aunt might be stirring.

As she crossed the yard she could see that the kitchen door was wide open, and could hear Hallie moving about. Confident that she could slip through the room while Hallie was in the pantry Faith noiselessly made her way to the open door and peered in. It proved a fortunate moment, for Hallie's broad back was turned as she moved toward the pantry; and, holding her breath in fear that the negro woman might turn and discover her, Faith tiptoed across the kitchen and reached the hallway in safety, and in a few moments was standing breathless, but triumphant over her success, in her own room.

"You Really Mean To Help Me?"

She had barely time to pull off her cap and jacket when Ellen, not yet fully awake, called sleepily:

"Oh, Faith! What are you up so early for? Mother won't call us because it's my birthday. Come back to bed," and she was again asleep before her cousin had time to reply to this welcome suggestion, and to quickly avail herself of it, grateful indeed for this chance to rest. Her last waking thought was of the sheltered cave which she was sure would be a safe refuge for the deserter. Nor could Faith possibly imagine that by her impulsive kindness toward this helpless man she had won a friend for the cause of American freedom who was, before many weeks had passed, to render a service which the people of Rhode Island would ever gratefully remember.

"Wake up, Faith! Mother has called us, and we are late for breakfast," and Ellen pulled back the blankets from her sleepy cousin, reminding her that it was the day of the eventful birthday party.

"I don't know what has happened to Hallie," Ellen continued as Faith reluctantly slipped from the comfortable bed, "but she was making a great outcry, and Mark, too. I heard him call out that robbers had been in the house," and Ellen chuckled with amusement at such an apparently absurd idea.

"Robbers?" Faith echoed.

"Oh, he couldn't find his boots," laughed Ellen, "as if anyone would carry off those old things;" and again urging her cousin to make haste Ellen hurried off, eager to discover the real cause of Hallie's excited outcry.

"They can't find out," Faith told herself as she quickly made ready to follow her cousin, and as she entered the kitchen she heard her uncle say:

"You'll probably find your boots, Mark. And as for Hallie's excitement about a few eggs and apples and a missing basket those things have happened before. There's no trace of a robber. Eat your breakfast, girls, and good luck and a happy birthday, Ellen," he concluded, giving his daughter a kiss as she clasped his arm; and for the moment nothing more was said of Hallie's outcry.

As Ellen turned toward the table she gave an exclamation of delight as she discovered a number of packages in her chair.

"Presents!" she declared, and the others smiled as the little girl unwrapped a bundle.

"It's a sash! It's lovely!" she whispered as she carefully unrolled a wide length of soft rose-colored silk with heavily fringed ends.

"It's one I had when I was about your age, Ellen. If you take as good care of it as I have perhaps you can pass it on to another girl some day," said Mrs. Morley.

"Oh, I never will! I'll always keep it!" Ellen promptly responded, and then again exclaimed as she lifted a square box of polished wood from the chair and set it on the table.

"It's a workbox! 'From Father and Mark,'" she read aloud from the slip of paper tucked under its lid; "and my name carved on top, and the date!"

"That is chiefly Mark's work," said Mr. Morley. "I furnished the wood; that's about all I can claim, except the threads and scissors inside."

Ellen and Faith were sure that no other girl in Newport possessed so fine a workbox. It was carefully lined with soft leather, with little loops for the scissors, and pockets for a good assortment of threads; and Ellen assured her father and brother that it was what she had wanted more than anything else, and did not notice that Faith had slipped from the room.

Running upstairs Faith opened the top drawer of her bureau, took out a little worn leather case and hurried back to the kitchen, and as Ellen turned toward her Faith held it out to her.

There was a little silence as Ellen opened the case and held up a string of pale pink coral beads. They all knew that Faith treasured these, a gift from an English aunt whom she had never seen, and Faith was the first to speak.

"They'll be just right with your pink sash, Ellie," she declared with such evident satisfaction in bestowing them on her cousin that instantly they were all sure that Faith was as happy as Ellen could possibly be in this gift.

"Porridge all cold," muttered Hallie, hovering near the table, and at this reminder Ellen and Faith remembered the waiting breakfast. The birthday gifts were carried into the sitting room, and the cousins took their seats at the table, while the rest of the family went about their daily work.

"The coral beads are best of all, Faith," Ellen earnestly declared, "and you can wear them whenever you want to. I'll wear them this afternoon first!" and Faith, well pleased that she had thought of the beads, and talking happily of the surprise Letty Stevens had promised them, forgot all about the deserter whom she had promised to help.

The day proved unusually warm for the season, and Mrs. Morley agreed that Ellen and Faith should wear their best gowns to the party that afternoon; and Mark was told to be ready to escort the girls to the Stevens' house which stood on Thames Street, not far from the Liberty Tree, dedicated in opposition to England's Stamp Act in 1766, by the Sons of Liberty.

Mark was still grumbling over the loss of his boots when the cousins started on their walk to Thames Street.

"But you have another pair, Mark, and much better ones than those old fishing boots," Faith reminded him. "Maybe that deserter those soldiers were searching for hadn't any boots at all."

"Well, losing mine won't help that fellow. I'd give them to him if I thought they would be of any use in his getting away from the British," Mark declared, and was amazed by Faith's exclamation of delight:

"Would you truly, Mark? Oh, that's splendid!"

"Well! Maybe you think he's got them. Perhaps he has, and Hallie's chicken and apples, too! Why, I never thought of the deserter! I'll wager 'twas he!" and Mark's eyes brightened at the thought that perhaps his lost boots would be of service in defying British rule.

But Ellen's laughter at such an idea made her brother acknowledge that it was not likely such a visitor could have escaped discovery; and bidding the girls good-bye at the door of the Stevens' house Mark started off toward Long Wharf, hoping to hear the rumors, which every day ran through the town, of the plans of the American General Spencer to drive the British invaders from Newport.

Before Ellen could reach for the brass knocker on the Stevens' door it swung open and she was greeted by a chorus of: "Happy birthday, Ellen," and she and Faith were drawn into the big hallway with the excited group circling about them.

Letty Stevens, her smooth dark curls tied back with a wide bow of scarlet ribbon, and wearing a ruffled gown of soft crimson delaine, helped Faith and Ellen to remove their capes and hats and then led the way to the long room at the right of the hall, and in a moment the treasured music-box tinkled out the gay notes of a minuet and Lucy Atwater exclaimed:

"'Tis the very tune the British band played last night at General Prescott's dinner party. Jane and I saw all the fine officers when they came down the street," and she nodded smilingly at Faith, as if sure that any news of Brigadier-General Richard Prescott was well worth hearing.

"I'd well like to hear an American band play a quick step to send the British marching out of Newport," declared Mary Clement, whose father and brother were with the army of Washington. There was a little murmur of approval from the other girls, but Letty quickly suggested:

"Let's dance. Take your places, girls," and curtseying to Ellen, she led the way and the girls promptly took their places, their full ruffled skirts fluttering grace-fully as they smilingly bowed and curtsied to each other in the movements of the dance.

Letty now clasped Mary Clement by the hand and said:

"Will you all please excuse Mary and me for just a moment? I'll be right back," and the group gave a little murmur of wondering assent as Letty and Mary left the room.

"It's the surprise," Ellen declared.

"And Mary knows about it," added Wealthy Richards, and the girls gazed at each other with little questioning smiles. But before there was time for them to make any expression of what the "surprise "might be, Letty was standing in the doorway.

"I hope you are all going to like my 'surprise.' It's all

ready now," she said, and the girls followed her into a large square room where stood a row of chairs that faced toward a corner, now hidden by a long curtain. Directly in front of this curtain stood a table.

Letty, sitting between Faith and Ellen, turned to smile at the girls behind her, and when Wealthy whispered: "Where's Mary?" she responded, "I guess you'll know in a minute," and they all gave a sudden start as the clear notes of a flute echoed through the room, and there were instant exclamations and gay laughter, as Lucy Atwater declared: "That's Mary!"

Then there was a buzz of delighted wonder when two tiny figures appeared on the table, bowed to the audience, and then to each other and promptly began to move jerkily about in a clumsy dance. Their faces were black, they each wore turbans of yellow cotton. One was dressed in a full white skirt and crimson bodice, and the other in blue trousers and a white coat. Their brief dance ended, they bowed again and disappeared as the girls loudly applauded.

In a moment the flute again was heard, this time in the gay strains of "Yankee Doodle," a tune that in years to come was ever to be associated with the triumph of the untrained American soldiers over the well-equipped British forces. As it ended two more figures stepped out from behind the folds of the curtain. These were much larger than those of the clumsy dancers. One wore a red coat with gilt epaulets on its shoulders, and carried a sword. The other was dressed as a sailor, with a "pirate's cap" twisted about its head. And instantly these two figures lurched toward each other in what was evidently a mortal combat, in which the sailor was promptly successful in battering down the red-coated soldier, and then pushing the fallen foe behind the curtain.

There was a horrified exclamation at this from Jane Atwater, but it was hardly noticed in the laughter and applause of the other girls.

"The next one is specially for you, Ellen," Letty whispered as a fairylike figure was now seen standing against the dark curtain. It was dressed in veil-like white, with filmy wings at its shoulders, and a crown of gilt stars on its head. There was a murmur of admiration, then a voice, clearly that of Mary Clement, but so low that the girls had to listen intently, repeated:

> "What's a birthday? 'Tis a time
> Set apart for joy and rhyme.
> Ellen, now we wish for you
> All good things in friendship true."

"'Lovely! Lovely!" they all exclaimed, and as Mary stepped out from behind the curtain the girls gathered about her with eager questions about the tiny figures which had given them so much pleasure.

"Mary and I made them ourselves," Letty proudly declared. "Mother helped us fix the strings to make them move about. Mary did that behind the curtain."

"Mary can do anything," Wealthy announced. "Why, she made a dress for her sister, didn't you, Mary? "

Mary nodded soberly. She was a year older than the other girls; and since her father and brother, with other Newport men, had left home to join Washington's Army, the family had had a difficult time, and Mary often felt herself too old for play as she had so many serious things to think of.

She and Letty Stevens were close friends, and Letty was always on the alert to share every pleasure with her friend.

Before the girls had ceased examining the clever little puppets Mrs. Stevens came into the room, and they all turned to greet her as she bade Letty lead the way with Ellen to the dining-room, where the table was spread for the birthday treat. And, although Hallie would have declared that the plain round cake, which Ellen cut with smiling satisfaction, was "no kind of a birthday cake," because it was without fruit or spices, Letty's guests had no fault to find with it, nor with the cups of cocoa, and the tiny biscuit that were served with it.

"It's been the nicest party," Ellen happily declared as the time came for them to go home, and the others all echoed this, saying they meant to make puppets for some future entertainment.

Mark was at the gate waiting to walk home with them; and before Ellen could begin the story of

Letty's wonderful surprise he was telling them the news he had heard at Long Wharf, news that made Faith tremble with fear as she listened.

CHAPTER IV

"GENERAL PRESCOTT is making a great fuss over that deserter those soldiers were searching for along the ledges. He says he is sure that someone must be helping the fellow, giving him food and hiding him, and that if he finds out who it is he means to hang him," said Mark, as they turned toward home.

"How can he find out?" asked Ellen, while Faith gave a little gasp of terror at the dangers in which she was now involved.

"Oh, he has spies lurking everywhere. And there are printed notices posted. Look! Here's one of them," Mark replied, pointing to a wall where a printed bill was fastened. They stopped in front of it, and Mark read it aloud:

"TAKE DUE NOTICE," it was headed in large black letters, then the deserter's name, Hugh Ramsay, followed by a description of the man, and then:

"Any person aiding this deserter in any way, with food, clothing or shelter, with advice or any manner of assistance, thereby becomes an enemy against His Majesty King George the Third and the British Government, and will be punished accordingly."

47

"Well, if anybody does help the deserter General Prescott won't find it out," Ellen declared, and at once began describing the puppets, and asking Mark if he would help her make some. "We could make one of General Prescott," she said.

Mark was at once interested in the idea; and as the brother and sister made plans for a set of puppets with which General Washington should overthrow King George the Third, Faith walked slowly on behind them wondering how she could continue to aid the deserter without being discovered. For notwithstanding the threats of the British officer the little girl was resolved not to fail the helpless man who had called her his only friend.

The road they were following now brought them to the turn of Mary and Clarke Streets, where stood the home of William Vernon, whose patriotic services to the cause of America's freedom from the injustice of British rule made him well known to everyone in the New England Colonies. It was largely due to his efforts that an American Navy was being formed to battle against the enemy. He gave his entire time, at great personal sacrifices and without payment, for the good of his country, and to establish its rights and liberty on a firm and lasting basis; and now, as Faith and her cousins passed the fine mansion, Mark exclaimed:

"'Tis enough to make us all rebels to see the British flag flying over Mr. Vernon's house, and to know that

Prescott's officers are quartered there," and he pointed to the English flag that floated over the dwelling.

The sun was setting when they reached the slope leading up to the Morley house.

Faith was so quiet that night that her aunt wondered if the little girl had failed to enjoy the afternoon; but as the family gathered about the supper table and Mr. Morley began talking of new troubles that the British were inflicting on the people of Newport, no one questioned her.

"It is said Earl Percy will soon return to England. That will give General Prescott full control, and things will be even worse for us. I want you children to keep more closely at home, and when you encounter any of the English soldiers be very careful what replies you make to their questions. You, Mark, must keep away from the wharves after this," said Mr. Morley.

"I'd well like to set their ships adrift," declared Mark, "and I believe it could be done."

"How could it be done, Mark?" Faith asked with so much eagerness that the others smiled, and Mr. Morley said:

"That's what General Washington would like to know, my dear. Boston succeeded in clearing its harbor of the enemy's fleet, and now they control Philadelphia, New York and Newport. If you can think of some way to clear Newport Bay of the British war vessels a good part of our troubles will end."

"File off their anchor chains some stormy night; that would do the trick," said Mark, and Faith smiled approvingly.

"I had thought of that," she soberly announced, and her aunt laughingly declared that it was plain enough that the warships would soon vanish.

Long before daylight of the following morning Faith vas again on her way to the ledges with a basket of food. But now a new surprise was in store for her. Hugh Ramsey was not there; nor did any trace of him remain in the rocky nook where he had found shelter.

Faith gazed anxiously about, hardly believing it possible that the man could have gained strength to leave. She discovered her blue flannel cape, neatly folded, and with a smooth rock holding it down securely.

For a moment she was sure that he had been discovered by Prescott's soldiers, but the folded cape reassured her, and picking it up she now retraced her steps as quickly as possible, and reached home before anyone was stirring in the Morley house. She returned the food to Hallie's pantry, crept up the stairs, and was able to slip noiselessly into bed without awakening Ellen, and with a sense of relief the little girl told herself that she had done all she could for the deserter.

"I hope he's safe. But probably I'll never know what becomes of him," was her last waking thought as she drifted into sound slumber.

But in this she was mistaken. She was later on to hear of him, and to be glad indeed that by her timely help she had made his escape possible. For, after days of constant peril of capture, of hunger and hardship, the man had succeeded in reaching the camp of an American regiment stationed at Tiverton, under the command of Colonel Joseph Stanton. Here he formed a friendship with a soldier named William Barton, and the result of this friendship was to cause a great sensation in Newport, and make General Prescott the victim of Yankee courage and cleverness.

Faith awoke the next morning in such good spirits that even Ellen wondered at the change until Faith gaily announced:

"Your birthday isn't really over yet, Ellen. I have a surprise for you almost as good as Letty's. Just as soon as we finish our morning work I'll show you," and she would only shake her head laughingly and respond: "Wait, you can never guess," although Ellen continued to ask questions and excitedly wonder what this new surprise could be.

"Oh, dear! It takes forever this morning to finish making the beds," Ellen declared; "and then we have to dust the sitting-room. 'Twill be noon before I find out what your secret is. It don't seem fair to make me wait that long," she pleaded.

But by the middle of the forenoon the girls had completed their usual tasks, and in response to Faith's smiling "All ready to start," Ellen pulled on her knitted cap and they ran down the slope to the shore.

"Oh, Faith! Is it that you have found where the pirates hid their gold?" Ellen demanded, as her cousin led the way up the ledge and stopped near the twisted oak tree that hid the entrance to the cave.

"Follow me," Faith commanded, and pushing aside the twisted branches she lowered herself into the cave, cautioning Ellen to watch her step, and in a moment the two girls were standing in the shadowy room.

The strong March sunlight filtered through the opening and sent its gleams along the green boughs that lined the walls; and the fragrance of fir and spruce mingling with the breath of the sea air gave the place an added charm.

"It's really your birthday present, Ellen. And it is to be our secret place. No one else, not even Mark, is to know about it," Faith said, with a little questioning glance at her cousin, half fearful that, after all, Ellen might be disappointed in the "surprise."

But Ellen's instant exclamation of delight and wonder as she gazed about, noticing the couch of heaped up seaweed, and the rocky shelf at the end of the cave, assured Faith that her plan was a success.

"We must have a name for it, Faith. So when we want to speak of it before other people no one but ourselves will know what we mean. What shall we call it? It must be something different from any other name," Ellen earnestly declared, seating herself on the pile of seaweed and looking about with such evident satisfaction that Faith felt well repaid for her work; and the two girls at once began suggesting names for this new possession.

"We might call it 'Refuge,'" said Faith.

But Ellen shook her head. "That sounds like a place for deserters," she responded. "We must have a sort of queer name. You ought to think of something, Faith, since you discovered it."

"'Verrazano'!" Faith exclaimed. "Don't you remember, Ellen? When your mother read us that book about Narragansett Bay? It is the name of the man who cruised along these shores in 1524. Aunt Cynthia told us to remember it. And he called it 'Rhode Island,' because its shape reminded him of the Island of Rhodes, and—"

But Faith's further information was ended by Ellen's exclamation:

"Oh, Faith! 'Tis just the right name. Nobody could possibly guess what it means. And we must have names for ourselves, and there they are! 'Verra' and 'Zano'! I'll be 'Verra' and you 'Zano'!" and the girls laughed happily over their decision; and from that time began a new way of addressing each other that, to their great delight, puzzled and amused their family and friends, and made Mark sniff scornfully at what he called their "silly talk."

"And this will be a splendid place for us to have puppet shows, just for practice," suggested Faith, as, with a last glance about the cave, the girls realized it was nearly time for the noonday meal and started for home.

That afternoon when the girls were ready for their lesson hour Faith asked her Aunt Cynthia so many questions about the early days of Narragansett Bay, and regarding its discovery by adventurous explorers, that Mrs. Morley again read to them a chapter of Rhode Island's history.

"Of course you both remember that the Indian name for this colony was 'Aquidneck,'" she reminded them, "and you know that Narragansett Bay is the outlet for three Rhode Island rivers—the Blackstone, the Woonasquatucket, and the Pawtuxet. And the bay has had a number of different names. One explorer called it the Bay of Refuge, and early mapmakers marked it as the Bay of St. Juan Baptist. Now I'll read what Verrazano wrote about this region to the King of France in 1524," and Mrs. Morley opened the book, wondering to herself at the girls' unexpected interest in the history of the colony.

"'We discovered an island of triangular form, about ten miles from the mainland, in size about equal to the Island of Rhodes, having many hills covered with trees. This region is situated in the parallel of Rome, being 41 degrees 40 minutes of north latitude, but being much colder.

"'It looks toward the south, on which side the harbor is half a league broad; a very large bay, in which are five small islands, of great fertility and beauty. Among these islands any fleet, however large, might ride safely, without fear of tempest or other dangers.'"

"Just as the British fleet does now," said Faith.

"But there is a tradition that Verrazano was not the first European to visit our harbor," continued Mrs. Morley. "'Tis said Leif, son of Eric, sailed from Greenland in the tenth century, and passed a winter on these shores, and that his Norsemen built the old Stone Mill.

"That is enough history for today," she concluded. "Now you can work out the problems in arithmetic," and the two girls, their thoughts still dwelling on their secret cave, picked up their pencils and applied themselves to the task; but Ellen glancing out to the lane exclaimed:

"Oh! Here comes Mary Clement and Letty Stevens!" and a moment later "Verra" and "Zano" were at the front door to welcome their friends.

CHAPTER V

Ellen's first impulse after greeting Mary and Letty was to tell them of Faith's discovery of the cave, but she fortunately remembered her vow of secrecy in time; and, wondering at the evident excitement of these unexpected visitors, she forgot for the moment all about the plans she and Faith had made.

Mary Clement, usually so quiet, now exclaimed eagerly:

"Oh, Faith! Ellen! Can you not come right over to my house? Ask your mother, Ellen. And hurry! Letty and I ran most of the way here! Oh!" and Mary sank down on the doorstone as if too exhausted to say more.

"We'll tell you about it on the way back. Run, Ellen, and ask your mother," said Letty; and as Mrs. Morley now came toward the door she was greeted by a chorus of eager voices:

"May we go to town with Mary and Letty?" from Faith and Ellen, and Letty's "Please say 'yes,' Mistress Morley, and we must start back this minute."

For a moment Mrs. Morley hesitated, then with a smiling nod she gave her consent, saying:

"Mary, you must see to it that my girls are safely home by sunset."

"Yes, indeed I will," Mary promptly agreed; and Faith and Ellen quickly seized their capes and hats and the little group ran down the lane toward the road leading to Newport.

"The other girls, Wealthy and Jane and Lucy are all at Mary's now waiting for us," said Letty, "and we were bound you shouldn't miss it."

"'Miss' what, Letty? You haven't told us anything. Have the British set fire to Redwood Library, or what has happened?" exclaimed Faith.

"The British are cutting down our Liberty Tree," Mary announced. And at this Ellen and Faith came to a full stop and gazed at their companions in such evident amazement that Letty gave a little giggle of delight as she seized Faith's arm and drew her along.

"'Tis a wonder they waited so long," said Mary. "Lucy Atwater came over and told us, and Mother said for us to remember it always. General Prescott is there on Thames Street, watching the redcoats chop it down."

For a few moments the girls hastened on without speaking, and soon turned into Thames Street and now walked on more sedately, for the road was filled by numbers of red-coated soldiers who kept a threatening watch over groups of citizens who gathered at nearby houses to sadly watch the downfall of this tree, their emblem of opposition to British rule.

It had been planted in 1766 by the Sons of Liberty, as a monument against England's Stamp Act that inflicted unjust taxation upon the American Colonies; and every boy and girl in Newport knew its history and now resented its destruction.

As the girls made their way toward the Clement house they overheard many resentful murmurs from the women and children who stood in doorways, and saw two red-coated soldiers marching off a group of boys who had shouted:

"We'll plant one you can't cut down."

Wealthy Richards opened the front door for Mary and her friends, saying:

"Mary, your mother says we can watch from the front windows. 'Twill fall in a minute!"

And now, silent and troubled, the girls gathered in the window and waited for the crash that would again prove the power of the British invaders.

"Why didn't somebody stop them!" exclaimed Ellen, as a cheer led by General Prescott echoed along the narrow street and the tree sank to the earth.

For a few moments Mary and her companions watched the soldiers, as they quickly trimmed off the limbs of the tree and began to saw its length into logs.

"I'm going to get a piece of the wood," declared Faith. "They shan't have it all."

"Good for you, Faith. Let's all go and get bits of it,"

said Mary; and even Lucy and Jane Atwater, whose family were known to be upholders of Tory rule, followed Mary and Faith as they led the way down the steps and across the street.

"We won't ask anybody's permission. It's our tree," said Wealthy, as they stepped over a broken bough and began gathering up bits of the smooth chips. Faith seized a stout chunk of wood that had been clumsily cut from the trunk of the tree, and the other girls were equally busy.

But suddenly one of the redcoats turned from his work and called:

"Here! You young rebels! Drop that wood and be off with you! We didn't chop down this tree to furnish you with kindlings."

"Run, girls!" Mary commanded, and holding fast the bits they had secured, the girls fled back to the shelter of the Clement house.

Lucy and Jane, who at the soldier's command had promptly dropped their bits of wood, now declared they must go home; and bidding the others a hurried good-bye they started off.

"It's time we were on our way," said Faith. "Aunt Cynthia will be looking for us."

"What will you do with your wood, Faith? I'm going to mark mine 'Chips from Newport's Liberty Tree,' and put them away in a box," said Wealthy.

"Faith has enough wood to make a box," said Mary,

with a smiling glance at the clumsy block that Faith held so firmly.

"Maybe I will make a box. I haven't thought yet what I will do," Faith responded.

"My pieces are only chips. I might as well throw them away," said Ellen, but at the chorus of exclamations that not a chip should be thrown away, she rather reluctantly put the bits into the deep pocket of her flannel gown; and, promising Mary and Wealthy that they would soon see them again, the two girls were off for their walk home.

There were still many loiterers along Thames Street. Groups of red-coated soldiers sauntered along as if confident of possessing the town. More than one questioning glance rested on Faith and the block of wood she was carrying, but the girls made their way on to the road leading near their home without meeting any acquaintance or being spoken to by passers-by.

The rattle of bridle chains and the beat of horses' hoofs made Faith and Ellen step quickly from the road, and they looked up at the group of English officers now close beside them.

The leader, mounted on a fine grey horse whose shining trappings caught the gleam of the descending sun, and whose plumed hat and immaculate boots and gloves proved him to be the "dandy" that he was so often termed, the girls instantly recognized as

General Richard Prescott. He glanced down at them, and, noticing the block of wood that Faith was carrying, drew rein and brought his horse to a standstill.

The big grey horse was so near to Faith that she moved quickly backward to escape the danger of his dancing sideway steps.

"Come here," commanded Prescott. "What wood is that you are carrying off?"

"Liberty wood," answered Faith, her blue eyes fixing their glance on the face that scowled down at her.

"Throw it down! Haven't you been taught any manners? Don't you know enough to curtsey when you meet your betters?" he said, bringing the dancing horse nearer to the undaunted girl.

"Yes, sir," she responded, "I do curtsey whenever 'tis right for me to."

There was a murmur of repressed laughter from the two young officers who accompanied the general, and he turned an angry glance toward them; for he never troubled to show politeness oven to his own household.

"I'll not be defied by even the children of this rebel town," he muttered as he started forward, apparently deciding not to waste further time on so small a rebel.

For a moment Faith and Ellen stood silently gazing after the vanishing horsemen; then they returned to the highway as Ellen exclaimed:

"Oh, Faith! However did you dare speak back to him? And you held on to that chunk of wood as if 'twas solid gold;" and, now confident that they were free from any further danger, the girls burst into laughter and began rapidly to rehearse their unexpected encounter with the British officer.

"I wish I'd been brave enough to speak to him," continued Ellen. "Why didn't we just begin and sing:

> 'Our land, the first garden of Liberty's tree,—
> It has been, and shall yet be, the land of the free.'"

"I don't know what would have happened to us if we had," Faith soberly responded, "and maybe your father won't like my answering General Prescott. I don't wonder his soldiers desert and run away."

"Father will say you were brave, Faith; you know he will," Ellen assured her, "and 'tis a fine story for Mark. He'll tell every boy in Newport that you were not afraid of General Prescott. Oh, haven't we a lot to tell when we get home!" and Ellen fairly danced along at the thought of the exciting story they could tell of the afternoon's happenings.

Mrs. Morley came down the lane to meet them, for the last rays of the setting sun were sending its gleams across the harbor, and she was glad to see them hurrying toward her.

"The Liberty Tree is cut down, Mother!" Ellen called. "That's why the girls came after us! We saw it fall," and she quickly told all that had so unexpectedly befallen them since they left home.

By the time they reached the house Mrs. Morley had heard the entire story of their adventurous experience, and had expressed enough amazement to satisfy even Ellen's demands. She smiled approvingly at Faith. "Your uncle will be well pleased by your courage, my dear; and I am glad indeed you held on to your block of Liberty wood. I wonder Prescott's officers bear with him," she said as they entered the house.

"Let's set the wood on the dining-room table, Faith," suggested Ellen, "and put my chips around it for Father and Mark to see, and then you tell about it."

But Mr. Morley and Mark had already heard of the destruction of the tree from a passer-by. They listened to the story the girls had to tell of their encounter with the British general with such evident satisfaction at Faith's courageous behavior that the little girl felt it was a day she would always remember.

That night she carried the treasured block of wood to her room and put it in the chest where she kept a precious doll, a small tea-set, and a wonderful glass ball which showed every color of the rainbow when held toward the light.

Mark had promptly offered to make a box for her from the wood.

"Can't I make it?" she had responded. "I'd like to," and Mark had somewhat reluctantly agreed. He had a box of fine tools and took great care of them; no

one else in the household was ever permitted to open
Mark's tool chest, so his agreement to allow Faith to
use them in making a box of the Liberty wood proved
how great an impression his cousin's adventure had
made upon him.

Faith was eager to at once begin work on the box,
but Mark said that the wood must "season" before
being shaped into any article; and bade her to let it
remain in the chest for a time; and, with the warmth
of the advancing spring, there was garden work for
the girls to do, the cave to visit, and so much to occupy
their time and thoughts that the Liberty wood was for
a time forgotten.

Matters for the townspeople of Newport were not
improving; but they had hopeful news of the suc-
cesses of the American privateers in capturing British
vessels laden with stores for the enemy. Newport had
furnished more seamen for the American fleet than
any other port save Boston; and Rhode Island had
furnished sixty-five of the ships that cruised the high
seas, with Abraham Whipple in command of the little
fleet; so that news of its exploits were eagerly welcomed by the undaunted residents of the town.

There was also encouraging news that the French
nation might send ships to aid the cause of American
independence; and this rumor gave new courage to
the Newport people. They realized that the only hope
of dislodging the British forces was by an attack from
the sea; and Rhode Island that had been the first to

put an armed vessel afloat against British aggression, in 1775, was now confident that it would not be long before Newport harbor would be cleared of British war vessels.

Ellen and Faith listened eagerly when Mark declared that some fine day there would be a sudden attack on the English ships.

"And we'll see them scuttle away fast enough. The ledge above our cove will be a fine place to watch them go," he said.

"Verrazano!" Ellen and Faith both exclaimed.

"You girls keep saying those heathenish words that don't mean a thing, responded Mark, for whom the name of the early explorer had no meaning.

"It's too bad not to tell Mark about the cave," said Ellen, as her brother stalked away.

But Faith shook her head. "We can't tell anyone, Ellen. We promised not to," she quickly rejoined.

CHAPTER VI

HERO

In the days following Faith's encounter with General Prescott she and Ellen found amusement in many visits to the secret cave, and carried there a variety of articles which they believed would add to their comfort if they ever fled to it as a place of refuge.

They cleansed and polished a number of clamshells, as Ellen declared these could be used as dishes for food; and they managed to construct a clumsy table from driftwood which they found along the shore.

As they now called each other "Verra" and "Zano" whenever they were playing about the sandy cove or along the ledge, and often when at home, the family became accustomed to the names and paid little attention to them save for Mark's muttered exclamations of: "Silly talk." Nevertheless he wondered at their air of evident secrecy, and why they spent so much time at the sandy cove; and more than once his unexpected appearance on the ledge made the girls wary of approaching the entrance to the cave without looking carefully about to make sure no one was to be seen.

More than once Faith's shrill whistle, three times

repeated, had warned Ellen not to push aside the rough branches of the oak tree; or Ellen's sudden call: "Verrazano!" had sent Faith scrambling along the sandy beach, so that when Mark discovered them they would apparently be gazing out at the warships, or searching for the tiny pink shells that could be found at the water's edge.

But one day in May, just after the departure of the kindly Earl Percy for England, the two girls, busying themselves happily in the cave arranging the clamshells on the rocky shelf, and talking of various possibilities that might send the British fleeing from Newport, their secret was nearly discovered.

"Verrazano," Faith whispered; and, as this had become a word of warning, Ellen instantly became silent; and, gazing toward the opening, the two girls listened to the sound of steps as of someone endeavoring to climb the ledge as noiselessly as possible.

But to do this was no easy matter; a pebble would crunch under the most cautious step, a bit of rock would become detached and roll against another, and it was these sounds that had reached Faith's ears as Mark made his careful way along the ledge and stopped near the oak tree.

Not venturing even to whisper to each other the girls nodded and pointed toward the entrance, wondering to themselves if it was Mark or one of the dreaded redcoats; and after a few minutes' silence

Faith ventured to tiptoe silently to where she could peer through the branches.

"Mark!" she whispered noiselessly, turning toward Ellen, and instantly the two girls were nearly overcome with the impulse of laughter; and, putting their hands over their mouths, they crouched down on the rock floor fearful that they would betray their secret by some noise that might cause Mark to find them out.

"Wonder where they went. I saw them come up this ledge," Mark said, as he seated himself on the same rock where the two soldiers had rested on that March day when Faith had been there.

But his thoughts soon wandered from the possibility of discovering their hiding place; for as his glance turned toward the harbor he discovered a boat putting out from one of the warships and apparently headed directly toward the ledge; and recalling how many farms had been stripped of their possessions, of cows butchered to provide meat for the British invaders; chickens, corn, and pigs and all provisions they could secure carried off by boats that scoured the shores for this purpose, Mark was instantly on the alert.

"They shan't get our cows," Mark exclaimed. "Ellen and Faith must help me," and he sprang up so quickly that a shower of rocks went rattling down the ledge as he ran swiftly toward the cove.

"What is it? What sent him off?" the girls asked each

other, and they crept out from under the branches of the oak tree in time to see Mark racing along the beach toward home, and to quickly discover the long-boat, rowed by stalwart seamen, nearing the shore, and at once understood Mark's exclamation.

"They are going to land here, Ellen! Whatever can we do to stop them?" and Faith jumped from rock to rock as if ready to plunge into the sea.

"Throw rocks at them!" Ellen declared, her blue eyes shining with wrath, and her yellow hair dancing about her face.

"Come on, 'Zano.' We can hide just above where they mean to land, and there are plenty of rocks. Maybe we can sink their old boat," and, with Faith close behind her, Ellen darted along the ledge to the shelter of a crag that overhung the water, and where broken bits of the ledge furnished a good supply to hurl at the rapidly approaching boat.

"If we could only push this crag over right onto their boat," said Faith, as she crouched beside Ellen in the shelter of the crag.

"Maybe we can," Ellen responded, giving a strong push against a part of the outstanding ledge.

"Look, 'Zano'! It moved! If we both push against it, it will surely fall!" she exclaimed.

"Not now! Wait until we are sure they mean to land here," she added, as Faith made ready to hurl herself against the unstable piece of ledge.

The boat was now so near that the girls could hear the oars against the rowlocks, and the commands of the young officer at the tiller as he directed the course.

"Here's deep water beside that crag, and a good enough place to land," they heard him say; and with bated breath, their hands pressed firmly against the tottering rock, the two girls waited for the boat to swing along until it was close beside the ledge.

"Now!" whispered Ellen; and putting forth all their strength the two girls pressed against the crumbling crag.

For a moment it hardly seemed to move, then with a sudden lurch it toppled over, striking the boat with such force as to instantly overturn it, and sending its crew, shouting their terrified surprise, into the deep water.

But the girls had not waited to see the result of the effort they had made. The moment the rock began to move they turned and ran up the ledge, hurrying to the protection of the cave. Neither of them spoke a word until they were safely in its shelter. Sinking down on the couch of seaweed they exchanged a look of triumphant delight.

"They can't carry off all our food and the cows now," said Ellen; "it will be all they can do to get ashore."

"They won't drown, will they?" and Faith was instantly on her feet as if ready to be off to the rescue of her enemies.

"Of course they won't," Ellen declared with such assurance that Faith again seated herself. "They are used to salt water. It will just give them a good soaking and teach them to keep away from this shore," Ellen confidently continued; and they decided that they must stay quietly where they were until sure that the sailors had departed.

Secure at "Verrazano" the girls had no knowledge of the result of their successful attempt to prevent the landing of the British sailors. The great rock hurtling into the boat had knocked over two of the men, leaving them stunned and bruised, and thrust itself through the bottom of the boat, so that when the surprised men got their heads above water it had sunk below the surface of the harbor.

It was a bruised and amazed crew who finally got themselves and their two injured companions safely on shore.

"Small use to try and conquer a people when their very rocks attack you," declared the young officer who had guided the craft, wringing the water from his short jacket.

"That rock was pushed down on us," said one of the men. "'Twas done on purpose," and he looked threateningly about as he added, "They meant to kill us."

"'Tis a bad place along these ledges, haunted by dead pirates, some say. We'd done better to take the other side of the harbor," muttered another.

"We'll get a warm welcome for losing that boat when we get back to the ship, if we ever do get back," said a third.

"'Tis easy enough to get back," replied the captain. "We are not more than a mile or so from the wharves where there'll be boats enough to set us aboard, and the sooner we start the better," and, helping the injured sailors to make their slow way down the ledge, the little group of seamen moved along the beach, crossed a stretch of pastureland and entered the rough road that led to Newport, little imagining that their raiding expedition had been defeated by the cleverness and courage of two small maids.

From a hiding place among the spruce trees the amazed Mark watched their departure. He had fled home with the news of their approach, and the family had promptly made every possible attempt to secure their property against what they felt sure was one of the raiding parties sent out from the British fleet.

The livestock had been hurried into hiding places long prepared for just this possibility, food and other articles had been swiftly concealed, and Hallie, armed with a sharp carving knife, stood in the kitchen door declaring that no thieving redcoat should enter her domain.

"Where are the girls?" Mrs. Morley had more than once anxiously demanded; and at last had told Mark to go in search of them.

"Be careful and not let these men see you; and keep the girls away until the fellows are gone," warned his father as Mark started off.

Keeping well in the shadow of the spruce trees Mark had nearly reached the shore when he discovered the struggling line of men moving across the rough pasture.

"What's happened? They're off, and look as if they had been pitched into the sea," he exclaimed aloud; and, forgetting all fear of being seen, he ran toward the shore, expecting at every moment to discover an overturned boat on or near the beach.

But there was no boat in sight. The ripple of the tide as it crept up the sand was the only sound he could hear. The waters of the harbor stretched calm and blue before him, with no sign that a stout craft had been sunk at the foot of the ledge since his last visit.

Calling the girls' names he now made his way to the ledge.

"Maybe they saw what happened. I'll wager they are well frightened, and hiding away behind some rock," he told himself, and was suddenly startled when he caught sight of his sister crawling out from beneath the old oak and with Faith close behind her.

"Are they all gone?" Ellen questioned fearfully.

"We sank their boat," Faith announced, brushing her hair back from her flushed face.

"Yes, we did. We pushed a great rock right down into it," Ellen confirmed.

"Come on, Mark! We'll show you just where it was. We saw they were going to land and we got behind the rock and pushed and pushed, both of us, and over it went, and then we ran—" Faith was about to add "to the cave," when Ellen's sudden "Verrazano" made her pause.

For a moment Mark made no response. That his cousin and sister had actually accomplished so great an undertaking seemed an impossibility; but they were both so serious, save for that silly word they were always saying, that he began to believe them, and listened to their story in grave silence until they reached the crag and Ellen gleefully pointed out where the outstanding rock had been pushed from its resting place.

"Well! I believe you really did get the best of that crew. What will Father say to this? He'll think you girls are as good as a regiment of American soldiers," Mark declared, with a smile of such triumphant admiration that Ellen and Faith grinned delightedly.

"I hope they all got ashore," Faith said.

"No fear. You couldn't drown those fellows," Mark assured her, as he peered down into the water hoping to discover where the boat lay.

Faith stood beside him and, hearing a whimpering noise that seemed to come from where the ledge sloped to the water, she gazed in that direction, half fearing to discover that one of the crew of the sunken boat might lie there, hurt and suffering because of her action against the raiders.

The whimper was repeated, and now Mark and Ellen both heard it, and Mark exclaimed:

"Look! There's a dog on those rocks," and he was off at the same instant with the girls close behind him.

Moving cautiously over the slippery ledge they were quickly near a crevice where lay a brown spaniel, who lifted a pleading gaze toward them and yelped frantically as he struggled to climb up the rocks, only to fall back, whimpering his dismay.

"He must have been in the boat with those fellows. I believe one of his legs is broken. Poor chap, I'll have you out of that in a moment," Mark promised, and kneeling down he reached into the crevice and gathered the suffering little creature into his arms.

The spaniel made no resistance. Its coat was dripping with water, and one of its forelegs hung helpless over Mark's arm.

"Father will set that leg all right," said Mark, and they all forgot for the moment their recent triumph over the boatload of British sailors in their excited interest over the injured dog.

"Will we keep him, Mark?" Ellen asked, half fearful that her brother would say the dog must in some way be restored to its former owners.

"Of course we will keep him; and take good care of him, too," Mark promised. "You girls can name him;

you seem to know all sorts of queer words," and Ellen and Faith at once began to suggest possible names.

But Mark shook his head at "Brownie," at "Star," and at "Sailor," and before they reached home it was decided to ask Mrs. Morley to give the dog a name.

The amazement of the Morleys and Hallie over the story the girls had to tell may well be imagined; and as Mr. Morley prepared splints and bandages and carefully set the broken bones of the whimpering dog, he questioned the girls as to the number of men in the boat, and praised them for so quickly acting to prevent a landing.

"I only hope Prescott does not send men along the shore and try to raise the boat," he said. "We'd not be apt to have so fortunate an escape in that case."

The little dog, with his curly coat now well dried, his injuries carefully attended to, and comforted by many pats and admiring words, now lay on a thick rug in a corner of Hallie's kitchen, and Mrs. Morley declared he had borne his misfortunes like a hero.

"'Hero'! That's the very name for him," exclaimed Faith, and they all agreed that no better name could possibly be found for this unexpected guest.

"I think 'Hero' should belong to the girls," Mark handsomely announced. "He's sort of a reward for their courage. I guess no other girls in the colony have defeated a boatload of British sailors."

"You must all keep this affair of sinking the boat a complete secret. If news of it reached Newport we would all be made prisoners, our house burned to the ground, and every measure taken against us. Remember this, every one of you. Don't speak of it to any human being," commanded Mr. Morley, and the family all agreed that the act that undoubtedly had served to protect their home, must never come to the knowledge of other people.

"It's been a more wonderful day than my birthday," Ellen declared that night.

"And 'Hero' is our dog," responded Faith. "Lots of things happen to us, don't they, Ellen?"

CHAPTER VII

MAJOR BARTON'S PLAN

Hallie regarded "Hero" as if he had deliberately planned an escape from the British, and was often heard praising him for finding his way to an American household. She tempted his appetite with tender bits of chicken, gave him saucers of milk, and kept a bowl of cool water ready for him. She brushed his silky brown coat, and so pampered and cared for him that in a short time the dog regained his good spirits, and made his way briskly about the house and yard in spite of his well-splinted and bandaged leg.

He quickly learned to respond to his new name, and Faith, Ellen and Mark all declared him to be a marvel, and to think the defeated visit of the raiders a most fortunate event, since it brought "Hero" to their home.

For a week following the girls' adventure the entire household kept a sharp watch toward the harbor and along the shore, fearing that another of the enemy's boats might appear; and not until several weeks had passed did they begin to feel any sense of security.

In their frequent visits to the ledge the girls never failed to look in every direction before entering the cave; for, as Faith continually warned Ellen:

"Maybe one of those sailors took the chance to desert, and he may be somewhere about the rocks or hiding in our cave."

"You are always thinking about deserters; ever since my birthday, Faith. You fairly jump every time anyone says 'deserter,'" Ellen laughingly responded. "It's just as if you expected General Prescott to say you helped that man who escaped the time the soldiers stole our basket of lunch and Mark's flint and steel."

"I wonder if that man really did escape, or if he fell off another ledge and they found him," said Faith, with so sober an air that her cousin gazed at her wonderingly.

"'Another ledge'?" she repeated. "Why, do you think he fell off this one?"

"Not this one," rejoined Faith, "and maybe he got away safely;" and Ellen, now intent on rescuing an oar that the tide was bringing into the sandy cove, gave no more thought to her cousin's queer interest in the man who had escaped from Prescott's unfair treatment.

Ever since they had pushed the big rock down the ledge the girls, from time to time, had discovered some floating object from the wrecked boat, and these they would do their best to secure. Taking off their shoes and stockings they would wade out until they could grasp a floating oar, or an empty box or basket; and, although this generally resulted in their returning home in dripping skirts, Mrs. Morley did not forbid it.

She cautioned them to be careful not to slip, and that neither girl was to venture into the water alone; and, although more than once they had each made unlucky stumbles and got well soaked as a result, yet no serious harm had befallen them, and Mark declared that the three fine oars they had drawn ashore were worth more than one ducking.

As June passed the Morley household kept more and more closely at home, and Faith and Ellen's friends in Newport now seldom came to see them. For, with the departure of Earl Percy, General Richard Prescott's arbitrary rule pressed severely upon Newport's citizens. This British general was a man advanced in years, of small stature, and with a harsh and undisciplined temper, and punished all who resisted his demands with merciless severity.

Believing himself secure in possession of Newport he made himself comfortable in the fine Bannister mansion, at the corner of Spring and Pelham Streets, and often rode along the pleasant road toward the west to visit his Tory friends, the Overings; nor could the overbearing general even dream that, because a little American maid had aided the escape of one of his soldiers, he was soon to suffer the most humiliating experience of his life.

If Faith could have followed Hugh Ramsay on those March days when he made his difficult and dangerous way toward the Americans' camp at Tiverton she might have realized more fully what her courageous help had accomplished. Later on she was to hear him tell the story; how the clothing she brought him gave him new courage, and the flint and steel enabled him, when beyond reach of the searching parties, to cool the potatoes and secure some warmth against the piercing March winds.

On reaching Tiverton he had told Major William Barton, a young American officer, of his perilous adventure, and of the aid he had so fortunately received from a courageous little maid.

Major Barton questioned him closely about General Prescott; as to where the general lived, and what his diversions were; and hearing that he frequently rode alone to dine and spend the night with the Overing family, the young officer at once began planning a daring undertaking. He was familiar with all the countryside about Newport, and recalled the brook along a ravine near the Overing place; and the deserter could so carefully describe the location, and the position of the British troops stationed near it, that Barton now conceived a plan of surprising General Prescott on one of his visits at this place, and taking him prisoner.

It was an exposed position, about a mile from any body of soldiers, and the deserter declared that there were no patrols on the shore, and that the general felt so secure on these visits that he took no special measures to protect his safety; the only safeguard being an English warship that lay anchored opposite the Overing place, which was a mile from the shore.

Realizing that his plan must be kept profoundly secret, Barton did not mention it even to his brother officers. Not until he had carefully worked out his entire scheme did he approach his commanding officer, Colonel Stanton, and ask his permission to undertake the dangerous venture. Stanton promptly agreed, but cautioned his young officer not to confide the object of his expedition to anyone.

Barton, however, asked Captain Ebenezer Adams, and four other officers, if they would undertake a secret enterprise with him, and ask no questions. They all promptly agreed. Boats would be necessary, he told them; and in a few days five whaleboats, that would carry forty men, were in readiness.

So as the pleasant days of June passed, and General Prescott enjoyed his frequent visits with his friends, bullied his officers, and exacted careful salutes from the boys of Newport, his downfall was steadily approaching.

Along the pasture slopes and ravines blueberries and raspberries were ripening, and Faith and Ellen made many excursions in search of them, for the berries were eagerly welcomed by the household. Food supplies became more and more difficult to obtain as the British continued to hold the town; and, added to the many discomforts forced upon Newport's people by Prescott's rule, was the fear that they would soon suffer even greater privations; and although the Morley household was more fortunate than many others, as they still had their cows and hens, and raised a sufficient supply of vegetables, while Mark's fishing excursions gave the family an abundance of this food, Hallie constantly complained because of the lack of sugar, molasses, and white flour, and their store of treasured honey was rapidly disappearing.

She urged the girls to gather as many berries as possible, and the days of early July found Faith and Ellen going farther and farther afield to fill their baskets. Some days Mrs. Morley consented to their taking squares of corncake with them; they would lunch on these and berries with cool water from some spring or running brook, and not return home until late in the afternoon.

As they were cautioned to avoid going near any encampment of the enemy the girls sought out such pastures and ravines as were free from British patrols, and Mrs. Morley was not overanxious when they failed to reach home before sunset.

Severe thunderstorms kept them at home for a number of days in early July, and when the morning of July 9th dawned clear and fine Faith and Ellen made their plans for the longest excursion they had yet undertaken.

"There are raspberry bushes all along that ravine that runs down to the shore, and not a patrol any-where; only that old guard ship; and we can go in wading if we want to, and dig clams and roast them in the sand behind the rocks," Faith said, as she and Ellen made their preparations.

"If we only had Mark's flint and steel those soldiers carried off," Ellen responded, "but Hallie has an extra one. She'll let us take it if we promise to bring home quarts of raspberries."

Hallie readily agreed to this, and put a gener-ous supply of crisp corncake in their basket, and with "Hero" barking pleadingly to be taken along, regardless of the fact that his injured leg still made long walks too difficult for him, the girls waved their good-byes to Hallie, who approvingly watched their departure, and set forth on the longest excursion they had yet attempted; and which was to end for Faith in a new adventure which she was ever to recall as one of the most perilous experiences possible for a girl to encounter—an experience which centered about a piece of Yankee courage which proved one of the most widely known events of the American Revolution.

The warmth of the July day was tempered by a cool air from the sea that brought the pleasant fragrance of bayberry and of the sweet grass that grew along

the pasture slopes. Faith and Ellen, wearing dresses
of faded gingham, and sunbonnets which had long
ago passed their first crispness, were quickly beyond
sight of the house. Their legs were bare, for stockings
were now becoming a treasured possession as the
household's store of yarn was used up, and, with the
British controlling every way to secure necessities,
no new supply was to be obtained. Their shoes were
old and well mended, but protected their feet from
the rough ground, and the girls felt themselves well
equipped for their expedition.

"Hallie means to dry all the berries we get today,
so we can have them next winter," said Ellen, as they
climbed a stone wall, where a startled squirrel leaped
away at their approach.

"No raspberry jam or any jellies for us this year,"
Faith responded, "but Aunt Cynthia says we may get
some molasses."

"Molasses!" Ellen scornfully repeated, "and all
those Tories having everything they want. I'll wager
the Atwaters have their cupboard filled with all sorts
of goodies."

It was nearly noon when they reached the head of
the ravine, where a stream of clear water made its way
through the thick undergrowth and over rocks to the
shore.

"Let's not begin to pick berries until we have had
our luncheon," suggested Ellen. "We can take off our

shoes and wade down the brook to the shore, dig the clams and cook them; there'll be plenty of time, all the afternoon."

Faith readily agreed; and taking their shoes and putting them securely in Ellen's covered basket, they stepped into the shallow stream and, with frequent exclamations of delight at the coolness of the water, and an occasional stumble over some unseen rock, they made their way toward the shore.

Once or twice overhanging bushes caught at their skirts. "Just as if they meant to stop us," laughed Ellen, as they carefully set themselves free.

The ravine opened on a sandy cove so much like the one near their home that the girls at once looked about for familiar ledges, but here there were only huge rocks at one side of the cove and a wooded point of land on the other. They could see the British guard ship well offshore, and this reminded them that they must use great care in building their fire, so that it would not attract any attention from the enemy.

They decided not to put on their shoes until they were ready to pick berries. Faith was to build and care for the fire, and selecting a sheltered spot among the rocks, she began gathering bits of sticks and drift-wood; while Ellen secured a flat strip of wood with which she could dig the clams; and taking a broken old basket they had brought along for this very pur-pose, she ran along the beach toward the wooded point near which a bed of clams bordered the water's edge.

The girls had many times baked clams along the shore, but never before so far from home; and, as they now dug an opening near the fire and put the clams into the mass of steaming kelp and seaweed and pushed the hot rocks over them, they talked gaily of their journey down the ravine and of their plans for the long summer afternoon that stretched so pleasantly before them.

"'Zano,' truly, isn't this the best time we have had all summer?" Ellen happily exclaimed, as they put on their shoes and prepared to leave the shore and begin to fill their baskets.

"Zano" promptly agreed: "Everything is just right; and it won't take us long to get all the berries we want. I'll go up one side of the ravine and you take the other side, 'Verra.' We can call across the brook, and then we'll get the very best of the raspberries," and, making sure that the last spark of fire was extinguished, they picked up their baskets and turned toward the ravine.

The ripe fruit hung in thick clusters on the prickly stalks, and, pushing their way through tangled thickets, the girls called back and forth across the stream as they exulted over the size and ripeness of the berries.

But, each one becoming intent on filling her basket as rapidly as possible, they moved farther and farther apart, until only now and then one or the other would send their call, of a whistle three times repeated, across the ravine, and hearing a similar call in prompt response would go steadily on, assured that the other was safely within reach.

The long afternoon drew toward sunset as Ellen, her basket heaped with berries, found herself nearly at the head of the ravine, and again sent her call echoing along its tangled banks. But there was no answering response.

"'Zano' will be along in a minute," Ellen assured herself, and was glad to rest against a moss-covered log on a little grassy knoll near the place where earlier in the day the two girls had started to wade down the stream to the shore.

Looking off across the fields she could see the Overing house, and the tall trees beyond it, and remembered that the well-hated Prescott was often a visitor there. But even the thought of this British general did not trouble her. She felt well pleased with the day's excursion. She and Faith had enjoyed every minute of it, and Hallie yeas sure to be overjoyed by their well-filled baskets.

A half-hour passed before Ellen's whistle again sounded. No answer came. And now Ellen noticed that the sun was low in the western sky, and shadows were deepening along the rough slopes of the ravine.

"Wherever can Faith be?" she wondered. "We ought to have been halfway home by this time," and she now called, "Faith! Faith!" and again whistled as clearly and loudly as she could, gazing anxiously toward the thickets, and hoping to get a glimpse of her cousin's faded blue gingham among the underbrush.

"Surely she wouldn't start for home without me," thought the puzzled girl; "but maybe she would, just to give me a surprise, and wait for me at the stone wall," and, when further calls failed to bring any answer, Ellen decided that this was what her cousin had done.

"Maybe I'll catch up with her," thought Ellen, not ill-pleased at what she believed to be a sort of game of hide-and-seek; and taking up her basket she started off toward home, keeping a sharp watch for some glimpse of Faith, and without the slightest fear that any harm had befallen her. Not until she reached the old wall, halfway to her home, and failed to discover any sign of Faith did Ellen have any sense of anxiety; and even then she told herself that her cousin had hurried on so as to reach home before her.

The dusk of the July evening was now creeping over pastures and harbor, and when Ellen came in sight of the Morley house Mark was just starting out in search of the belated girls.

"Where's Faith? "Mark asked, as his sister came running toward him.

"Oh, she played a game with me; she's home before me," Ellen declared.

"Then she came some other path. She wasn't there when I left," Mark answered.

"Well, she must be home," his sister replied, as Mark took her basket and they hurried on together.

But Faith was not at home; nor had she attempted to play any game with Ellen.

Eager to secure the best of the raspberries, she had pushed her way further and further amongst the underbrush, circled a small ledge, and kept on until she filled her basket. Then, turning in what she supposed was the way toward the brook, she wandered on, surprised that no response came to her calls.

The dusk deepened over the thickets. The evening calls of song-sparrows and wood-thrush sounded from nearby bushes, and a heron's mournful cry echoed in the distance as Faith steadily pushed aside one tangled mass of vines after another. Not until the last glimmer of light had faded, and stars showed in the clear summer sky, did the girl realize that she must have been moving about in a circle, and that she had no idea of where she was.

"I'm lost!" she exclaimed aloud, "but Ellen must be trying to find me, and if I keep on calling and whistling she surely will," and the three long whistles again sounded through the thicket.

CHAPTER VIII

A BOLD ENTERPRISE

Faith now found herself back at the moss-covered ledge.

"I'd better stay here," she decided. "I don't know which way to go. Oh, I do wish I had a drink of water!" and with a little sigh of fatigue she sat down on the mossy ledge.

Her bare legs were scratched by the brambles, her worn skirt torn and soiled, and she discovered that she had lost the faded cotton sunbonnet. She could not see anything save the heavy shadows of the underbrush, and as she satisfied her hunger with the juicy ripe berries she listened hopefully for the echoing whistle that would tell her of Ellen's whereabouts; and not until an hour had passed did Faith fully realize that there was little hope of any rescue by Ellen.

"Maybe 'Verra' is lost too. Oh! I wish we had kept together. I don't know where I am. I can't hear the brook, and I don't know if I've been going toward the shore or toward the Overing house! Anyway, Uncle Morley and Mark will surely come and look for us. I'll whistle and shout, then they will find me," and, comforted by this decision, Faith rested back against

91

the sun-warmed ledge, resolved not to give way to her fatigue and the sleepiness that from moment to moment nearly overcame her.

But the long day in the open air, the constant movement, and her recent struggle through the thickets, had overtired her. Her head rested comfortably against a cushion of moss; the calls of the woodland birds died away, and she was quickly asleep.

The darkness of the summer night deepened. In the Overing house, not far from the ravine, General Richard Prescott made his comfortable preparations to retire, believing himself secure against any possible danger. A mile offshore lay the British guard ship; and creeping over the quiet waters of the harbor, under the favoring stars of the summer night, came a number of whaleboats manned by Americans and led by Major William Barton.

Each man was well aware of the perils and uncertainty of the expedition, and knew what his fate would be if they were discovered. With muffled oars they steered carefully between Prudence and Patience Islands, to avoid the enemy's ships; then keeping close to the west side of Prudence Island, safely rounded its southern end, going so near the British ships that they heard the sentinel's cry, "All's well," as they pulled noiselessly on.

Major Barton had carefully informed his companions as to the object of their undertaking: the capture of General Richard Prescott. He had cautioned them to preserve the strictest order; to observe profound silence; and on reaching the Overing house, if they were so fortunate as to escape discovery, not in any way to injure the house, to have no thought of plundering the enemy.

The forty loyal Americans heartily agreed to this, and swept rapidly on toward the shore at the foot of the ravine. So silently did they land that even if Faith had been watchfully awake she would not have heard them.

A man was left in charge of each of the boats, while the rest of the party made their way along the deep gully toward the Overing house. Barton's negro servant kept close behind his master as they moved noiselessly on. The deserter had told Major Barton that there was sure to be a sentinel stationed near the house, and that Prescott's aide, Major Barrington, always accompanied him on these visits, and that Mr. Overing and his son would surely be in the house, besides other members of the family and a number of servants.

They could not avoid the sentinel; but, advancing noiselessly upon him, seized his musket and made him a prisoner. The house was now quickly reached, and every door guarded by the Americans. Barton and the negro forced open the front entrance and the surprised Prescott was made a prisoner before he had time to dress.

No one of the household made any effort to protect

him. Major Barrington, at the first alarm, had leaped from his chamber-window, only to be seized by the watchful Americans.

There was no time to lose. There was sure to be an instant alarm that would arouse all the British forces; and rather carrying than leading the captured Prescott, and urging on the sentinel and Major Barrington, they dashed toward the shore through the thickets, and so near to the mossy ledge where Faith rested that she awoke with a sudden cry of terror.

"What's this!" exclaimed one of the men, almost as alarmed as the startled girl, and hesitating a moment at the sight of a little figure appearing out of the darkness.

"I'm lost! Are you British soldiers?" Faith managed to say.

"Lost, are you? Well, I've no time now to bother with you. But follow on; we are bound for the shore;" and, in spite of knowing that even a moment's delay might menace his safety, he reached a friendly hand toward her and drew her on beside him as he ran after his companions.

"We've captured Prescott," he joyously exclaimed as he hurried her along. "What do you think of that, little maid? Will you know how to get home when we get to the shore?"

"Oh, you are Americans! Yes, I'll know how to get home! Oh, where is General Prescott?" Faith excitedly demanded.

"Ahead there! That bundle those men are carrying," he responded.

There was no time to say more. The shore was now in sight, and with a hurried "Good luck to you, little maid," the man darted ahead to join his companions; and Faith, still clutching her basket, watched the group of exultant Americans as they hurried their prisoners into the waiting boats and pushed off.

Almost instantly alarms were sounded. The explosion of muskets, the loud warning of bells, and shrill trumpet-calls aroused the British army; yet no pursuit was made. No one could tell the way the Americans had taken; and not until the following day, when Barton sent word that their commander was safely a prisoner in Providence, did Prescott's officers know what had become of him.

For a time Faith crouched among the rocks where, a few hours earlier, she and Ellen had so happily eaten their clams and corn bread. But she was now too excited by her recent encounter to think of that, or that she was alone on this strange shore in the darkest hours of the night.

She smiled as she recalled her glimpse of the captive general.

"The soldier called him a 'bundle,' and the men were almost carrying him along. I wish Mark could have seen them," she thought, peering through the darkness into which the boats had so quickly disappeared.

She no longer dared to call or whistle. "I might bring a whole British regiment after me," she told herself, with a delighted chuckle over the success of the Americans. She no longer felt the slightest inclination to sleep; and as soon as the light of early dawn began to creep up the sky Faith was on her feet ready to start for home.

This time she did not go up the ravine, but made her way across pastures and through a small growth of woodland.

As she emerged from the woods she heard someone calling, "Faith! Faith!"

"That's Mark! Here I am," she called back, and ran forward to meet her cousin and uncle.

"Ellen lost me," she announced, "and I got all turned around in a thicket and went to sleep. And when I woke up a lot of Americans were running past me on their way to the shore. They had taken General Prescott prisoner. And I saw him, and he looked like a bundle," and, out of breath, Faith gazed up at her uncle's anxious face and quickly added:

"Did Ellen get home?"

"Yes, and expected to find you there before her," Mark responded. "We have been out all night; but Ellen couldn't tell us where to look for you. She thought you must be near the old stone wall."

"Then you didn't see any of the men who captured General Prescott! Oh, Mark! I wish you had seen them! And when their boats left the shore there wasn't a sound. And then right away the English began to fire muskets and ring bells! Put the boats slid off into the dark."

As Faith finished her uncle exclaimed:

"Do you really mean that Prescott has been captured and carried away, and that you saw it?"

"Why, yes, Uncle Morley," and Faith now related clearly what had befallen her, and told of the friendly man who had helped her on her way to the shore.

"It's almost too good news to be true," declared Mr. Morley, as they now came in sight of the house where Mrs. Morley, Ellen and Hallie were anxiously awaiting them.

"Prescott's captured!" Mark shouted, and in the excitement over this great news, and the fact that Faith had seen him carried off, no one save Aunt Cynthia noticed that the little girl seemed hardly able to stand.

"Never mind about Prescott; Faith must go straight to bed. Hallie, heat a bowl of milk and bring it upstairs," and putting her arm about the tired girl, assuring her that she and Ellen could talk later on, Mrs. Morley helped her to her room, and Faith was quickly in bed.

Hallie brought the warm milk and she drank it gratefully.

"Don't wake up for hours," her aunt smilingly said.

"You know the rhyme your uncle repeats about the three best physicians:

   'First Dr. Quiet,
   Then Dr. Restawhile,
   And Dr. Diet.'

You'll need them all for a few days," and Faith was too tired to even respond as she sank back against the pillows and was quickly asleep.

When she awoke it was well past midday, and already the news of the capture of General Richard Prescott, by Major William Barton and his soldiers, was being repeated along every highway, and a passer-by had confirmed the story Faith had so excitedly related.

Wherever the news spread, it made a great impression. Every American welcomed it as a hopeful sign of an early triumph over the invaders of Newport; and Major Barton was warmly praised and commended for his bold enterprise. Later on he was to receive a vote of thanks from the General Assembly, who also ordered that each man who had accompanied Barton should receive a reward of money.

Besides this Barton was advanced in rank and made a Brevet Colonel in the Continental Army, and Congress voted him a fine sword engraved with his name and the record of his courageous undertaking.

As Faith opened her eyes Ellen appeared in the doorway with "Hero" close at her heels.

"Oh, 'Zano'! Are you really awake? Mother says you had best stay in bed until you are really rested, and I'll bring up your dinner. There's a fine chowder," and Ellen gazed anxiously at her cousin, half afraid that Faith might be too tired to want food.

But she was now wide awake. "I'm going to get up this minute. Ellen! Did I dream about General Prescott, or is it true that Americans carried him off from the Overing house?"

"It's true, 'Zano'! And you saw them!" Ellen eagerly responded. "I'll bring you up some hot water, and you are to put on your pink gingham," and Ellen was off to the kitchen with the good news that Faith was awake and ready to get up. "Hero" did not follow her but came trotting across the room, put his paws against the bed, and with his silky head tilted to one side, gazed at her as if he realized that she had recently been in peril.

"Oh, 'Hero'! You are the best of all the Britishers," declared Faith, smoothing his silky ears, and the brown spaniel barked delightedly at her approval.

He was now freed from the splints on his legs; and, well cared for and petted by all the Morley household, felt himself quite at home. Usually he kept as close to Mark as possible, but he was always eager to follow the girls on their excursions after berries and along the shore.

Ellen now appeared carrying a big brown pitcher filled with hot water.

"I'll come back and brush your hair if you want me to, 'Zano,'" she suggested; it seemed to Ellen that her cousin had been through a wonderful experience, and was entitled to almost as much consideration as Major Barton himself.

Faith promptly refused this unusual attention; and Ellen, with "Hero" trotting after her, was off to the kitchen to make sure that the "fine chowder" would be ready.

Faith dressed herself more carefully than usual; the clean fresh garments and soft cotton stockings seemed of more importance than ever before; and as she put on the faded pink gingham dress, she gazed at it admiringly.

"It's prettier faded," she decided, and ran downstairs eager for her belated dinner.

Hallie and Mrs. Morley, and Mark and Ellen were all in the kitchen, and as Faith ate the steaming chowder, followed by the hot corn bread which Hallie had baked on purpose for her, Mark asked her many questions regarding the number of men she had seen.

"'Tis a pity you didn't wake up in time to follow them up to the house," he said, when Faith owned that she had only seen groups of silent men hurrying their prisoners to the shore.

"I went to town this morning," Mark continued, "and all Newport is telling that no one at Overings' made any resistance. Prescott's aide, Major Barrington, jumped out of his chamber-window. I'd like well to have seen him," chuckled Mark.

"And there is talk now that General Spencer means soon to start a drive against the British, and send them out of Rhode Island. If he does, Faith, you will probably be on hand; you have all the luck," concluded Mark, as his cousin finished her corn bread, and Hallie soberly reminded the girls that the raspberries must be picked over and spread to dry in the attic.

"But your basket ain't of much account this time, Miss Fathie. Jest a few berries in the bottom. Not as I'm blaming you, pore lamb; I knows you had to eat 'em," the negro woman soberly declared.

As the days went on Mark brought further news from Newport regarding Prescott's capture.

"A deserter put Barton up to it, 'tis said. A fellow who escaped last spring, and made his way to Tiverton. Perhaps it was the very fellow those soldiers were after when they stole our food the day we went fishing," Mark told the girls a week after Faith's night in the ravine.

"Maybe it was the deserter who took the food. I hope it was, and that it helped him to escape," said Ellen.

"I'd well like my flint and steel that they carried of," Mark rejoined.

But Faith had nothing to say. She was earnestly hoping that Mark was right; and that the man to whom, at no small risk to her own safety, she had carried food and clothing, had indeed been the one whose information had led Major Barton to conceive and carry out the bold enterprise of capturing the British general, one of the boldest and most successful adventures of the American Revolution.

"It would be just as if I myself had helped," she thought, recalling the half-starved man who had called her his "only friend."

CHAPTER IX

A WINTER'S CELEBRATION

Within a month after the eventful night of July 9th, 1777, the American boys of Newport were singing clever verses regarding Prescott's capture. They took good care however to keep beyond reach of the wrathful British officers as they sang:

"Go to King George and to him say,
  Call home your troops, call them away,
  Or Prescott's fate they'll share;
  For Barton, with his sling and stone,
  Will bring the great Goliath down
  And catch him in a snare."

Mark sang it joyfully, and Faith and Ellen quickly learned the lines; even Hallie chanted the words as she went about her work.

As September approached there were many rumors among Newport's patriotic people that General Spencer, then in command of American troops in Rhode Island, would soon make an attempt to drive the enemy from their stronghold. At this time the British force numbered about four thousand well-trained soldiers, the greater part of whom were stationed in or near Newport. Four regiments were on Windmill Hill, and others in control of the ferries, and their position was very strong. With British warships in Newport harbor there seemed but a small chance that any attempt could succeed against them unless an attack could be made by sea; but this, in September of 1777, seemed impossible.

Nevertheless in October General Spencer assembled nearly nine thousand men at Tiverton in readiness for such a venture; and many of Newport's citizens were preparing to aid in this effort to free their port from their unwelcome visitors.

But it proved an unfortunate undertaking. A sufficient number of boats could not be secured, and a protracted storm so discouraged the men that many refused to make the attempt, and at last the plan was given up, bringing disappointment and loss of prestige to Spencer, who soon after resigned his command. He was succeeded by Major-General John Sullivan, whose courage and ability were well known throughout the colony.

The Morley household heard various rumors, but as the autumn of 1777 advanced and winter drew near they began to be less hopeful, and to be seriously concerned as to how sufficient food could be obtained. Many people were leaving Newport for the mainland, fearing the severe conditions they would have to endure with the coming of winter.

Through the summer months Mr. Morley and Mark had caught a good supply of fish which they dried on shelf-like rests in the hot sun. When thoroughly cured the fish were stacked safely away in a dry loft. A pig was killed, and the hams put in the smokehouse; and from their garden they stored potatoes, cabbages and other winter vegetables.

Their flourishing hives of bees gave them a quantity of honey, and with the dried berries and apples they felt themselves better off than most of the American families. But it became more and more difficult to secure corn meal, and it was months since they could obtain any wheat flour.

The girls in Newport with whom Faith and Ellen had enjoyed so many pleasant parties were now kept closely at home. The Atwater family had removed to New York, and the Clements and Stevens families lived, as did the Morleys, in constant fear of even worse privations than they had yet endured.

So as the winter advanced, with fierce storms and ice-bound shores, the Morley children busied themselves indoors; and, remembering the "puppets" of Letty Stevens' party, Ellen easily persuaded Mark to bring his treasured tool chest into the warm kitchen, and with a good stock of well-seasoned pine wood, and with Hallie exclaiming over their cleverness, they carved and whittled a number of tiny figures from the soft wood; and Ellen and Faith, with bits of colored wool and silk, made proper uniforms for the soldier puppets and ruffled gowns for the ladies.

As each little figure was completed they would give it a name. "General Prescott," in a coat made of red flannel with high epaulets of twisted gilt braid, a tin sword hanging from his belt, and a cocked hat of white cotton, gave them a chance to again sing of his capture; another puppet was called "Major Barton," and the largest and finest was named Washington. Dressed in a blue coat, with white breeches and a blue and white cockade on his hat, the leader of the American forces stood inches higher than his companions, and was treated with the respect that every mention of his name was always to evoke from loyal Americans.

Ellen insisted on a puppet of Lady Washington, and another to be called Mistress Dorothy Hancock, the wife of the patriotic John Hancock of Boston, Massachusetts, of whose beauty and accomplishments the girls had often been told.

As the cold winds whistled about the house, and snow piled up along walls and fences, the warm kitchen with its big fireplace heaped with glowing logs seemed a very pleasant place to Faith and her cousins as, gathered about the workbench that Mark had brought in from the shed, they carved the soft wood, or stitched the bright garments, making many hopeful plans for a visit from Mary Clement and Letty Stevens, which they meant to celebrate by surprising them with a puppet play.

Mary and Letty had promised to come for a day and spend the night, and all the Morley household were looking forward to the visit. It had been decided that if the second Monday in December should prove a day of good weather Mark would go to Newport to escort the girls to the Morley home.

"If it doesn't rain before then and melt the snow I'll take my sled and the girls can take turns riding on it," Mark handsomely declared. "There'll be no fine Prescott to stop us."

"But there's a new British general in Newport, Mark, Sir Roger Pigot. Didn't you hear Father say that this new general was more to be feared than Prescott?" said Ellen.

"Oh, that's because Pigot has put his soldiers to work building batteries near Fogland Ferry, and on Butt's Hill. Father meant that Pigot may make more trouble for our soldiers than Prescott did," Mark responded. "He isn't so anxious that every boy in Newport should pull off his cap to him, anyway."

When the last of the little figures was finished and the girls had completed their fine costumes, Faith and Ellen began to discuss the "play" for the puppets.

"We must have a name for it. And we had best write down just what each one is to say," Faith suggested.

"Let's call it 'Victory,'" Ellen excitedly exclaimed, "and have General and Lady Washington tell Mistress Dorothy Hancock that every British ship has left Newport harbor, and will never come back. And that American ships are bringing us lots of sugar and flour and everything."

"But that isn't true!" Faith soberly objected.

"Well, it's going to be true," insisted Ellen, "and, anyway, plays are just made up stories."

"What will we do with General Prescott?" rejoined Faith.

"Oh! We will have him kneel to Washington," laughed Ellen, and the two girls, well pleased at so easily deciding on their programme, now busied themselves with paper and pencils, writing down what each puppet would say on appearing on the little stage they meant to arrange in one corner of the living-room.

"I wish we could have the words rhyme," said Faith.

"Why not?" rejoined Ellen, to whom nothing appeared impossible. "You say a line, 'Zano,' then I'll say one to rhyme with it, and we'll write them down."

"Let's make a little figure like a fairy. Not out of wood, but twist those bits of lace over wire, with wings, and a crown of gilt paper; and have her come out first and introduce the other puppets," suggested Faith.

Ellen leaned back exclaiming: "'Zano'! That's perfectly splendid! Oh, you do think of just the best things! We'll make the fairy now!"

And pushing away paper and pencils the girls began again searching through Mrs. Morley's piece-bag for the bits of filmy lace they had seen there and for a roll of wire which had found its way into Mark's "handy box."

An old valentine furnished enough gilt paper for a tiny pointed crown; and before the early dusk of the December day began to darken the corners of the big kitchen the "Fairy Queen," holding a slender straw for a wand, stood complete on the table before them.

"She is the best of all, Faith! We must think of something lovely for her to say," declared Ellen.

Faith nodded in response, her thoughts circling round an old rhyme which her own mother used to repeat to her:

"A fairy is a winsome sight,
And ofttimes comes in dreams at night,
But seldom do you see at day
A happy fairy at her play."

"That won't do to recite," she told herself, "unless I can think of some rhyme to add to it;" and, after various attempts, to every one of which Ellen promptly gave admiring approval, they decided that the Fairy Queen should open their entertainment by repeating the verse, to which. Faith added these lines:

"But now a Fairy Queen will tell
 Of great and small, whom you know well."

Mr. and Mrs. Morley declared the puppets had been
very skillfully made. Mark had attached the arms to
the shoulder by clever "joints" of strips of leather,
and the knees were joined in the same way. "General
Prescott's knees will bend all right," Ellen announced,
as she held up the red-coated figure.

Wigs of raveled yarn completed the costumes, and
the "Fairy Queen" was the only puppet who could
stand upright without support.

The second Monday of December dawned clear
and bright. A slight crust had formed over the banks
of snow, and as Ellen and Faith peered from their
chamber-window that morning they exclaimed over
the silvery shining fields and pastures, and the snow-
tipped branches of the spruce trees that glittered in
the rays of the morning sun.

At an early hour Mark was ready to start. Wearing
his high moccasins, and with his flannel-lined coat,
wool mittens and knitted cap, he had no fear of the
biting wind that swept up from the icy shore; and
Ellen and Faith warmly dressed in woolen stockings
and stout shoes, over which their knitted leggings
were drawn, their coats tightly buttoned over their
flannel gowns, and wearing their quilted hoods and

warm mittens, were ready for the slide down the long slope which would be the start of Mark's journey to Newport.

"Go straight back to the house," Mark warned them, as the sled coasted to a standstill near the open pasture that Mark must cross before reaching the rough highway that led to the town.

"We'll be all right, and watching for you and the girls when you come back," said Faith, as they left the sled.

"I hope he doesn't meet any redcoats; they might take his sled away from him," she added as they turned toward home.

"They would have to catch him first. I'll wager Mark can outrun any of them," replied Faith.

If she wondered a little over Ellen's whispered conferences with Aunt Cynthia and Hallie, Faith nevertheless did not question her cousin; and there were still preparations to make for their visitors, so she gave little thought to Ellen's air of excited secrecy.

Mark found the streets of Newport more quiet than when he visited the town during the pleasant days of autumn. He passed the fine old State House, used as a hospital by the British. He saw that a number of houses had been torn down since his last visit. "More firewood for the soldiers," he told himself angrily, wondering if the entire town was to be finally destroyed by the enemy.

Mary Clement was ready and waiting his arrival; and, as they started down the street toward the Stevens' house she asked eagerly:

"Has Faith remembered about today?"

"Not yet," Mark smilingly responded; "she's been so taken up with having you and Letty for visitors that I don't believe she even knows the day of the month."

Letty's greeting was an excited question:

"Oh, Mark! Does Faith know about today?"

"Not a word, unless Ellen has told her since I left home," he rejoined.

"She wouldn't!" Mary and Letty promptly exclaimed.

But Mark shook his head. "Never can tell about girls," he declared.

CHAPTER X

A DECEMBER BIRTHDAY

Faith and Ellen were on the watch for the first sight of the expected visitors, and at the door to welcome them; and as Mary greeted Ellen, Faith overheard a half-whispered question: "Does Faith know?" and Ellen's excited response: "Hush, she may guess," and she followed the others into the warm living-room, again wondering to herself what the secret could be in which she had no part; and feeling that, after all, this long-expected visit was not going to be as joyful an occasion as she had expected.

As Mary and Letty warmed themselves before the glowing fire, taking off their leggings and quilted hoods, and talking eagerly of the events of their long walk from Newport, Faith could not fail to notice more than one whispered word between them and Ellen.

"And they keep looking at me as if they wished I wasn't here," she told herself, with an unhappy feeling of not being wanted, so that when her Aunt Cynthia came into the room to welcome Mary and Letty, and turned a smiling glance toward her niece, she was surprised at Faith's sober face.

"Come, my dear, you and I will go first," she said, clasping Faith's hand; and with the other girls, laughing and whispering together, they all moved toward the kitchen, where the long table had been moved to the center of the room, and where Mr. Morley and Mark were awaiting them.

Hallie, dishing up a large platter of fricasseed chicken, looked over her shoulder to smile widely and to nod her approval, as Faith, with a wondering at the well-spread table, noticed that one of the high-backed chairs was decorated with evergreens, and its seat heaped with packages.

"This is your seat, Faith, and a happy birthday to you," said her uncle, as he lifted the packages to the table and drew out the chair for the surprised girl who, with a gasp of amazement, repeated: "Birthday!" as the little group circled about her exclaiming laughingly over her failure to remember her own natal day.

"Don't open the packages until after dinner," her aunt suggested, noticing Hallie's gestures toward the table. "Mark will take them into the living-room."

Faith, now smiling happily, readily agreed, and took her seat between Letty and Mary, confessing that she had wondered at the whispers and glances she had seen them interchange with Ellen; and gazing admiringly at the shining damask tablecloth, "that Aunt Cynthia only uses for real company," she proudly remembered, and sent a radiant glance toward her well-pleased companions.

It was such a dinner as the Morley family had not enjoyed for a long time: besides the fricassee of chicken there was a big bowl of creamed onions, another of mashed turnips, as well as potatoes. There was milk to drink, and applesauce sweetened with honey. And when even Mark refused further helpings the smiling Hallie cleared the table, and set before Mrs. Morley a large glass bowl, at which Letty Stevens exclaimed:

"It looks like rose leaves heaped up with snow."

"It's 'raspberry fool,'" Ellen proudly announced.

And, as Mrs. Morley helped each one to a heaping saucer of the freshened berries covered with whipped cream, there were appreciative smiles and Faith said: "This is better than any birthday cake."

She was eager to open her birthday gifts; and, as the little group gathered about the table in the living-room, they all turned to watch her.

Mary Clement had made a dainty handkerchief with Faith's initials embroidered in one corner; Letty had brought a good-sized package of rock candy, a great treat in those days; and Mark and his father had made her a workbox exactly like Ellen's; while a pair of long blue wool stockings was a gift from her Aunt Cynthia and Ellen.

"I knit one and Mother knit one," said Ellen.

"And Hallie has something for you," said Mark, as the colored woman opened the door.

"Oh, Hallie, come and see all my fine presents!" exclaimed Faith, running to meet her and drawing her toward the table.

Hallie came smilingly forward, and her exclamations of admiration over the simple gifts made Faith even more confident that she was the most fortunate little maid in the colony of Rhode Island.

And now, from the depths of the deep pocket of her brown skirt, Hallie drew out a small round package and thrust it into Faith's hand, and the girl opened it eagerly.

"See! See!" she exclaimed excitedly, holding up a string of tiny blue beads; and, quickly slipping them over her head, she turned and clasped Hallie's arm with both hands, saying:

"They're lovely! Lovely, Hallie! I'll always keep them;" and Hallie, well pleased over the success of her gift, went smiling and chuckling back to the warm kitchen.

Mr. Morley and Mark soon left the room, and Mrs. Morley also turned toward the kitchen, leaving the four girls to chat happily for a while before the open fire.

Mary and Letty had much to tell of the doings of the British in Newport, of houses being torn down for firewood and churches used as stables and riding-schools.

"But General Washington is sure to drive them

away, just as he did from Boston," Mary confidently asserted.

"But when?" Ellen demanded. "Father said, months ago, when General Prescott was taken prisoner, that very soon we'd see the last of the enemy. But they are still here," and she gazed almost accusingly at her companions.

"We can't help it," Letty laughingly responded, "but perhaps we'll see that young French general, the Marquis de Lafayette, come with an army before this time next year, and drive off the British."

"'Next year,'" repeated Faith, in so disconsolate a tone that the other girls could not refrain from laughter. Mary Clement then gave them news of their friend, Wealthy Richards, who was shut indoors because of a sprained ankle.

The short December afternoon sped rapidly toward twilight, and when Mark appeared suggesting that they go to the kitchen and crack the walnuts and shadbarks that he had ready for them, the girls all thought it an added pleasure, and were quickly established near the big fireplace.

"Where is Mark?" questioned Letty, as he did not join then.

"Oh, he has to help Mother," Ellen promptly responded. For, before the arrival of the visitors, it had been decided that Mrs. Morley and Mark would arrange the tiny stage for the puppets in the corner of the living-room, and call Faith when all was ready for her to conceal herself behind the curtain, where she would manage the appearance and movements of the tiny figures by means of the slender sticks and strings Mark had so skillfully arranged.

Hallie was in the secret; and when the kitchen became shadowy, lighted only by the blaze of the dancing firelight, she called Faith, saying that her aunt wanted her; and Faith ran toward the living-room and quickly concealed herself behind the curtain.

The "Fairy Queen" was already on the stage, and as Mark led the girls into the room and Letty and Mary discovered the tiny shining figure they exclaimed in wondering delight.

The big room was dim with the deepening shadows of early evening, but at each side of the stage stood tall brass candlesticks casting a glow of light over the little platform; the window shades were drawn, the fire leaped and sparkled, and, as Mark set chairs for them and they all turned eagerly toward the stage, Ellen exclaimed:

"That is just the way fairies look!" with such conviction that the others laughed heartily. Then, at the sound of a low voice repeating: "A fairy is a winsome sight"—they were all quiet.

Faith's voice, low and measured, went on with the verse, and the lines she had added; then, to Ellen's delight, came other rhymes:

"Here a play you now will see
Of Washington and victory.
Like Prescott, Pigot soon will go,
And Newport peace and joy shall know."

As the low voice died away, and the "Fairy Queen" was wafted upward by a clever arrangement of unseen strings, the little audience loudly applauded, and Mr. Morley declared that Washington himself might well enjoy such an entertainment.

There was more applause when the red-coated puppet kneeled to Washington and Barton; and the elegant appearance of Lady Washington and Mistress Dorothy Hancock caused murmurs of admiration. Then, when Washington alone held the stage with the "Fairy Queen" hovering above him as if to crown him with all her gifts, the curtains were drawn together, and Faith appeared flushed and smiling to be praised and applauded by Mary and Letty.

"But 'tis Mark who did all the work," she promptly declared, "and Ellen who thought first of the fairy."

"But you made up the rhymes, 'Zano,'" rejoined Ellen.

"Why do you call her 'Zano'?" asked Letty.

"Oh, that is part of a secret. It really began on my birthday; and when my next birthday comes maybe you and Mary and Wealthy Richards will come, and then 'Zano' and I will have another surprise for you," Ellen smilingly replied.

It had been an exciting and happy day for the entire household. For a few hours even the older people had forgotten the hostile forces that spread terror and destruction over the colony of Rhode Island, and they all had a hopeful conviction that the "Victory" the puppets had announced might not be very far distant.

To Faith it was the happiest birthday she had yet known. She and Ellen lay long awake talking over the success of their puppet play, and the evident delight of their visitors; and Ellen suggested that her own birthday should be celebrated at "Verrazano," by taking Mary, Letty, and Wealthy into the secret, and introducing them to the hidden cave.

Faith readily agreed to this.

"Perhaps the British ships will all be gone by that time," she hopefully responded.

But no such speedy good fortune was in store for the patriots of Newport. The winter of 1778, on which they were just entering, was to prove a time of great privation and deep anxiety to all loyal citizens; and Faith's birthday was long remembered by the Morley household as the only carefree day of that severe winter.

Nevertheless General Washington was making plans to again endeavor to drive the enemy from Rhode Island. With General John Sullivan in command of the American troops stationed there, and with the Continental brigades, under the young French officer, the Marquis de Lafayette, which Washington would send to General Sullivan's aid, there was a hopeful chance of success.

Then, too, there were rumors that a French fleet might come with the spring and drive the British ships from Newport harbor. But as yet these rumors had no evidences of confirmation, and Newport citizens saw their churches, library, and homes injured and abused by the red-coated invaders, and were helpless to protect themselves.

Mary and Letty had promised to reach home by midday, and at an early hour on the day following the puppet show they were ready to start, with Faith and Ellen accompanying them down the slope.

"You can both ride 'til we get to the road," Mark told the visitors, as the solid crust made it easy for him to draw the sled over the snow-covered fields.

"A lovely visit!" Mary called back, as the sled went swiftly along, waving her mittened hand to Faith and Ellen who stood gazing after their departing guests.

"Lovely!" echoed Letty, and a moment later they disappeared beyond a growth of scrubby pine trees, and Ellen and Faith turned toward home.

"It's growing colder every minute," Ellen declared as they climbed the slope," and those dark clouds over the harbor surely mean more snow. I hope Mark gets home before it begins."

"Aunt Cynthia said we were to put the puppets away and set the living-room in order," Faith reminded her cousin as they reached the house; and taking off hoods, coats, and leggings, the two girls promptly busied themselves with their appointed work.

They had so many pleasant things to talk about that the morning hours sped swiftly by, and when Mark came rushing into the house declaring that snow was falling, and that he didn't believe they would see anyone from Newport again that winter, they could hardly believe that it was time for dinner.

"Leavings from yesterday," said Mark, with evident satisfaction, as they all gathered in the warm kitchen. "Wish some of us could have a birthday every week," he added, and began to tell of the groups of redcoats he had seen near the Redwood Library in Newport.

"It will be a sad pity if they injure that building or destroy the books," said Mrs. Morley; for the beautiful library, built in 1748, and generously endowed by Abraham Redwood, was regarded with pride by all the citizens of Newport.

"'Tis abused by the English officers now," Mark asserted. "They carry off the books in armfuls; and no American is allowed to even enter the building."

As the others talked Ellen's gaze was fixed on the snow that was being blown in gusts against the windows, and she remembered that her father and Mark had planned a journey to a wood lot, at some distance from the house, to bring home a load of firewood; and

Mr. Morley had promised the girls that they might ride on the sledge.

"We can't go after the wood today," she soberly remarked.

"'Twill clear before night ; 'tis too cold for a heavy snow," said Mr. Morley, "and we'll be off early tomorrow morning."

His prediction proved correct. There was a clear sunset, with flickers of red running up the western sky; and the two girls went happily to bed rejoicing in the prospect of riding on the rough wood sled over the snowy fields on the following morning.

"Wouldn't it be fun, 'Verra,' if we were going to take potatoes to roast, and build a fire, and have a winter picnic in the woods?" said Faith, as she prepared for bed.

"Well, 'Zano,' we can't have a party every day," Ellen soberly reminded her.

Nevertheless on the following morning Mr. Morley announced that he and Mark meant to bring a large load of wood. "We will have to shovel off a good bit of snow before we can begin loading the sledge; so if you girls want to go with us you must be prepared to stay until after midday," he said, as Faith and Ellen, wearing their warmest garments, followed him into the yard.

"We shall build a fire and cook bacon and potatoes for dinner," said Mark, smiling at the cries of delight that welcomed this statement.

Old Lion, the big grey horse, turned his head to look at his passengers as Ellen and Faith seated themselves on the wood sledge. Mark tucked an old blanket snugly about them, and waving a gay good-bye to Hallie, who watched their departure from the kitchen window, the little party was off.

They were all in good spirits, praising Old Lion and the sunny day; and looking forward to the delights of hours in the clear winter sunshine. Not even Mr. Morley had any anticipation of the dangers they were soon to encounter, nor of how sadly they would make their way home.

CHAPTER XI

As the sledge moved steadily on across pasture-land and snow-covered fields the two girls, warmly wrapped under the old blanket, looked down on the ice-bound harbor and caught sight of the fluttering flags of the English ships. But on this sunny December morning their thoughts were too happily occupied to even notice this evidence of the enemy's power.

They were eager to reach the long stretch of wood-land, and very soon the fragrance of its pine trees scented the clear air, and Mark jumped from the sled to lead Old Lion in among the trees along the rough wood road, now covered deep with snow. Sometimes the sledge tipped dangerously to one side over unseen rocks, and Faith and Ellen clutched at the stout poles of the cart with shouts of excited laughter, thinking it a splendid beginning for the woodland picnic.

Coming out in a wide clearing, where piles of snow-covered wood proved they had reached their destina-tion, Old Lion came to a standstill looking back over his shoulder as if to ask "what next?" and Mr. Morley and the girls were quickly off the sledge.

"Now, girls, you can do as you please until I call

you. But don't go far outside this clearing. Those old stumps would be a good place to eat our lunch, and you can clear the snow away from them and start a fire while Mark and I load the sledge," said Mr. Morley, adding:

"Here's my flint and steel. Take care and not lose it," and instantly the girls were off toward the center of the clearing where several mounds of snow showed the location of the stumps.

"If we had some sort of a broom we could clear off the snow in no time," said Faith.

"Well, then, we'll make brooms," was Ellen's laughing response; "plenty of branches on these little fir trees," and they turned toward the edge of the clearing breaking off the thick boughs from the small trees. With these they quickly cleared the snow from the old stumps, and, selecting one that showed rotten wood near the ground, they began preparations for the fire.

With the sharp end of the fir branches they dug out an opening in the decayed wood near the ground.

"It's all lovely punk. It will catch fire like paper," declared Ellen, as Faith carefully struck a spark and in a moment a tiny blaze was eating into the wood.

"It's just like a wooden fireplace," said Faith, as they warmed their hands. "Now we must clear a good place to roast the potatoes," and they began to sweep away the snow directly in front of the sturdy little blaze which was making good headway into the old pine stump, and soon had a circle of bare ground. Over this they piled a small heap of pine branches, and Mark brought them two chunks of dry wood that he had brought from home. Lighting this new fire with bits from the blazing stump it speedily blazed up, caught at the dry wood, and settled down into a steady fire, melting the snow around it in a widening space.

"There'll be a splendid lot of hot ashes for the potatoes, and we can cook the bacon over the stump," said Faith, as she and Ellen regarded the successful result of their efforts.

"Let's get armfuls of pine boughs and spread them around that big stump," suggested Ellen, pointing toward a smooth-topped stump nearby which they had cleared of snow, and which they had already decided to use for a table.

Leaving their fires burning steadily the two girls began breaking of branches from nearby trees, and spreading them in thick layers, making a carpet over the snow-covered ground.

"Lucky we wore our old mittens," said Faith, looking a little mournfully at her stained mittens, now sticky from contact with the rough bark.

By the time they had completed their "carpet" the fire had burned down to a bed of hot coals and a heap of glowing ashes. The girls had many times baked clams on the shore, and roasted potatoes on similar excursions; and, while Ellen went to the sledge to bring the basket that contained their food, Faith with a scrubby branch from a spruce tree brushed away the hot ashes, and with a sharp stick dug a small cavity where the frozen earth had been thoroughly warmed, so when Ellen arrived all was ready; the potatoes were dropped into the warm earth and covered with hot ashes on top of which were the still glowing coals, and over the coals more ashes.

"They'll be well cooked by the time Father and Mark are ready, and the stump is making a lovely fire for the bacon. And, Faith! Look! Hallie put in apples; we can roast those, too."

"And I brought part of the rock candy Lettie gave me," said Faith. "Mark will like that."

"Father will too," responded Ellen, jumping about on the springy branches of the pine carpet that surrounded the log.

"Oh, Faith! Isn't this splendid? Don't you think we have good times! That lovely party yesterday; and today off here in the woods is as good as a party. I'm not a bit cold, are you?"

"Not a bit. We are all shut in by the woods as if they were walls of a house, with the blue sky for a roof. Oh! What's that?" and Faith's startled glance followed the leaping figures of two white rabbits darting across the clearing.

"Rabbits. Didn't they look like snowballs? Something in the woods must have frightened them," Ellen rejoined.

As the girls moved briskly about in the clear air making preparations for the noonday meal Mr. Morley and Mark were busily at work loading the sledge with wood. Old Lion, freed from his harness and supplied with a bundle of hay they had brought for him, seemed to be well pleased with his lot as he now and then shook his head and stamped his feet as if to make sure that he was really free.

By the time the last log had been lifted to the sledge the potatoes were well cooked, and Mr. Morley and Mark, warmed thoroughly by their work, came hurrying across the clearing.

"I'll cook the bacon," said Mark, as he drew the thick slices from the paper in which Hallie had wrapped them, and took out the old iron frying-pan and set it to heat over the coals of the stump.

"There's a jug of ginger tea sweetened with honey—I saw Hallie mix it—and butter and salt for our potatoes," announced Ellen, as she and Faith brushed away the hot ashes and each one of the little group, with the aid of a pointed stick, secured a well-roasted potato.

The appetizing fragrance of the frying bacon gave then all a quickened sense of hunger; and, sitting on the pine boughs that the girls had spread about the stump, they were happily enjoying their meal when with a little scream Ellen jumped to her feet as a frightened rabbit bounded past her.

"Another rabbit!" she exclaimed. "Whatever makes them come running out of the woods as if they were being chased?"

"They are being chased! Look!" whispered Mark, and the others turned quickly to gaze toward the further end of the clearing.

For a moment they were all silent as three red-coated figures, each carrying a rifle, came out from the woods. The soldiers, evidently on a gunning excursion, seemed in the best of spirits; as they discovered Old Lion and the loaded sledge they called out:

"Here's luck. We'll drive back to the barracks in state," and now they came swiftly toward the little group gathered about the burning stump.

"What's this?" exclaimed the leader, sniffing at the smell of bacon, and looking wonderingly at the two girls, who, each with a red apple that they had just roasted over the coals of the dying fire, gazed at the newcomers in evident terror.

Mr. Morley, whose lameness made it difficult for him to rise quickly to his feet, was now standing, but he made no response.

"I could do with a bit of bacon myself," declared one of the soldiers, smiling at Mark.

"It's all gone," said Ellen. "We have eaten everything except the apples."

"Well, keep your apples, little maid," and he turned quickly to Mr. Morley.

"Hitch that horse to the wood sledge, and be quick about it. You rebels, with your good firewood, and lunching like lords," and he made an ugly thrust toward Mr. Morley.

Mark's first impulse had been to resist the invaders, but a whispered word from his father made him realize that any such movement would end in serious trouble, and he now followed Mr. Morley toward the wood sledge, where, urged on by the soldiers, they harnessed Old Lion to the sledge, both wondering what would be the fate of the horse, born and reared at the Morley farm, and used to kindly treatment.

Mark resolved to make an effort to save Old Lion; turning to the soldiers he said:

"You are welcome to the wood. I'll drive the sledge wherever you say."

"Mighty kind of you," laughed the young officer. "We'll drive ourselves. This horse is in good condition; he'll be useful to us. We'll look you people up later on, and find out where you get your bacon," and climbing to a seat on the loaded sledge, where his companions quickly followed him, they urged the heavily laden horse on across the clearing toward the place where they had first appeared.

Too frightened and surprised to speak Faith and Ellen had stood gazing at this scene, fearful that these redcoats might force Mr. Morley and Mark to accompany them. But as Old Lion disappeared among the trees Faith called out:

"They can't have Old Lion. Oh, Uncle Morley! Make them bring him back."

But her uncle shook his head. "Pick up the basket, girls. The frying-pan and jug are all we have to take home," he said.

"They shan't have Lion. I'll get him back some way," Mark declared, thinking angrily of all the hard work he had done in chopping down the trees and preparing them for firewood. "Just to keep our enemies warm," he muttered.

Mr. Morley was silent as they set forth on their long walk home. The loss of the sturdy horse was a great misfortune; besides that, the young officer's threat of looking them up would, if he succeeded, doubtless mean the loss of their supplies of food, possibly of valued household possessions.

Ellen and Faith plodded on behind Mark, hardly noticing the roughness of the way.

"Those first rabbits, 'Verra.' If we had only known what they meant, that they were being chased by redcoats, we might have started for home before they found us, and saved Old Lion," said Faith.

"They would have followed us, and that would have been even worse," Ellen gloomily responded.

The bright sunshine of the early morning and midday had vanished. Clouds were creeping over the sky, and a sharp wind came sweeping across the pastureland. Now and then spits of snow struck against their faces.

"I'll Get Old Lion Back Some Way"

"Keep close to Mark, girls," called Mr. Morley. "It's blowing up a storm, and we must do our best to get home before dark," and the little group that had set forth so gaily now plodded soberly on as the snow came down more and more thickly.

"They shan't have Old Lion. I'll find a way to get him home," Mark declared again.

"But you don't know where to look for him," said Faith.

And this was to prove sadly true. For, although Mark did his best to discover the whereabouts of the grey horse, he was unsuccessful. The Morleys were never again to see Old Lion.

Dusk had fallen long before they reached home; and Mrs. Morley and Hallie had set candles in the kitchen windows to light their way. A blazing fire burned on the wide hearth, and a steaming chowder was ready to welcome them; even the bad news they brought did not prevent Mrs. Morley from finding comfort in the fact that they were all safely at home.

"They might have made your father and Mark go with them," she told Ellen, as the little girl mourned over what had befallen them.

The girls were ready for bed at an early hour, thoroughly tired out by their woodland excursion and the long walk home. Not until the next morning did Faith remember that the package of rock candy had been entirely forgotten, and was still safe in the deep pocket of her woolen skirt.

Shut in by heavy snows the girls had no news of Mary Clement or Letty and Wealthy; but busy with their patchwork, for each was making a quilt of bits of gingham and calicos, and with their daily lessons and household work, the days passed rapidly; and they made many plans for the coming spring and for the March day that would bring Ellen's thirteenth birthday.

"Perhaps by that time Washington will have driven the English out of Newport," Faith hopefully declared. "Won't it be grand, 'Verra,' when we can go to our cave and not see those old warships in the harbor?"

CHAPTER XII

THIMBLE-BOXES

As the winter days passed and Mark failed to discover any trace of the valued grey horse the family resigned themselves to its loss; and as the weeks went on and they remained unmolested by the redcoats they regained a sense of security.

Faith, busy with her patchwork, sometimes thought of the day that now seemed so far distant, when she had discovered the deserter helpless among the ledges, and wondered if she might not now tell of that adventure.

"I guess I'd better not," she decided; "maybe he isn't safe yet."

She and Ellen recalled with satisfaction their successful effort to prevent the landing of the boat at their ledges, and Ellen declared that "Hero" was their reward for that courageous action.

The past year held so many events for the two girls that they were never at a loss for things to talk of and wonder about; and the puppets furnished them more than one evening's pleasure.

"Where is that block of Liberty wood you were going to make a box of, Faith?" Mark asked one stormy day in February. "It must be well seasoned by this time."

"Oh, it's safe in my chest. I'll get it," Faith responded, and was off through the chilly entry and up the stairs to her room before Mark could add that he would help her shape the treasured wood into a box.

"Here it is," she announced, holding out the clumsy chunk that she had rescued on the day the soldiers had cut down Newport's Liberty Tree, and when she and Ellen had encountered General Richard Prescott on their way home.

"I want to make the box myself, Mark," she continued. "Do you suppose I can?" and Faith's face was so grave and her voice so serious that Mark laughingly asked:

"Going to present it to General Washington?" and quickly added: "Of course you can make it yourself if you want to. If you'll be careful and do just as I tell you."

Faith nodded her agreement. "I'll be just as careful as I can," she promised.

"You had best let me split the wood into the right pieces," said Mark, carefully examining the block, and noticing the grain of the wood; and then selecting the proper chisel and knives from his tool chest as Faith, seated on his workbench, which had remained in the corner of the kitchen ever since they made the puppets, earnestly watched him.

"This wood will take a lot of work polishing," said

Mark, as he carefully split the block into smooth squares.

"I'll polish it," Ellen offered, but Faith shook her head.

"No, Ellen. I want to do it all myself, every bit of it. Why don't you make a box of the bits you brought home?"

"I will!" Ellen eagerly responded. "It will have to be a little one; about big enough for a thimble!"

"Why, Ellen! That's splendid. Whoever heard of a 'thimble-box'! Maybe I can make one, too," Faith rejoined, with an admiring glance at her cousin as she added: "You think of lovely things, 'Verra.'"

Mark was very patient and exact in helping the girls with the work. He showed Faith just what tools to use, and how to cut the corners of each square to fit securely. It was work that he enjoyed, and Ellen declared it much better fun than knitting or sewing.

Mrs. Morley was interested in Ellen's suggestion about thimble-boxes.

"Why not make a number of them? They would be nice gifts for your friends; and anyone would value a box made from wood of our Liberty Tree," she said as she watched the little group gathered about Mark's workbench.

"I'll make one for you, first of all, Mother," promised Ellen, "and then I can use bits of Faith's wood and make one for Mary, and Letty, and Wealthy. I'll give them to the girls on my birthday," and Faith and Mrs. Morley both declared this the happiest of ideas.

"March isn't so far off," Ellen contentedly announced one day in mid-February, as she gazed admiringly at the three tiny boxes she had already completed. "I do hope the snow goes quickly, and that my birthday is warm. Do you suppose our cave is all right, 'Zano'?"

"Of course it is. Caves can't run away," said Faith, industriously polishing the cover of her box. "We will have to do a lot to it, though, to make it right for a party."

"What are you going to do with your box, 'Zano'?" asked Ellen when it was finally completed, and the entire family gathered about to admire the careful workmanship and the tiny tree Faith had so skillfully carved on the cover.

"I am going to give it to General Washington when he drives the British away from Newport," Faith soberly responded.

"Well, if he knew about that he wouldn't lose any time," Mark laughingly asserted. Nevertheless, they all thought it quite the proper thing that Faith should want the great general of the American forces to have this box.

"Then I will give Lady Washington a thimble-box," said Ellen.

"Why not? I am sure she would prize it," Mrs. Morley said, and henceforth the two girls had a new interest in the hoped-for victory of their patriotic army.

It was a day in early March when Mark heard the first clear, loud whistle of the meadow lark, one of the first of springtime birds to start for its northern nesting ground.

"There's a flock of them in the spruce trees," he told the girls. "Come on, I'll show you where they are. But keep quiet, and don't go too near," he warned, as Faith and Ellen followed him down the slope toward the thick growth of spruce trees.

"There they go!" he exclaimed, as with a flutter of wings the little flock rose in the air, and near enough to the girls so they could plainly see the birds' brilliant yellow breasts with the black crescents and the white patches on the tails.

"That means that spring has really come; but the meadow larks never begin nesting until May. I wonder why they come so early;" said Mark, and reminded Faith and Ellen of the nests among the dried grass that they had discovered the previous year.

"The redwings will be along soon," Mark promised.

"And robins," added Ellen; and now every day brought fresh signs of springtime. The snow had disappeared; the shore and ledges were free from ice; and it was now possible for the cousins to visit their secret cave and to begin their preparations to celebrate Ellen's approaching birthday.

It had proved a quiet winter for the American troops stationed in Rhode Island. In Newport the

British officers amused themselves, as they had done in Boston and Philadelphia, by establishing a riding school in one of the churches; by dances, and theatrical performances in which the Tory residents were glad to join.

The loyal Americans continued to suffer under many privations, but were nevertheless resolute in their determination to withstand injustice and to overcome the enemy. From time to time Mark came home from his frequent visits to Newport with the tale of hopeful rumors. Among these was the report that General Sullivan planned to attack the British at Newport as soon as he could collect a sufficient force; and on the day before Ellen's birthday he came running up the slope toward the house in evident excitement.

"These old warships will be out of our harbor before you know it," he declared, meeting the girls, closely followed by "Hero," who were on the way to the shore.

"Tommy Mason's father says the French are going to send a fleet to help us, that they'll be here by early summer."

"Well, anybody would think you could see their sails now," said Ellen. "Early summer means June, and it's only March now," and Faith and Ellen went on their way but little impressed by what Mark considered the most wonderful news. Their thoughts were now centered on the surprise they were planning for their friends, and on making the secret cave as attractive as possible.

"It won't be a secret after today, so we might as well tell Mark about it," said Faith, as they climbed the ledge.

"And Mother and Father, too," responded Ellen., "and why don't we have a picnic dinner there? If it is as warm as today we could, and I know the girls would like it."

"Let's go right back and ask Aunt Cynthia if we may. Oh, 'Verra'! It will be fine," and the girls turned and ran up the slope toward the house, eager for Mrs. Morley's consent to this new plan.

"Why, yes. If it is reasonably warm I think we will all enjoy a few hours on the ledge. Hallie shall make us a chowder; and even if you can't have a cake, Ellen, you can have just as good a birthday," she said.

"Oh, I don't care anything about a cake! Faith and I have a surprise for everybody," Ellen declared, "and a picnic dinner will be just the thing."

"If it doesn't grow too cold," Faith soberly reminded her.

But the sun shone brightly the next morning, and by the time Mary, Letty and Wealthy arrived there was no doubt as to the warmth of the day; and the guests, led by Faith and Ellen, made their way along the shore and climbed the ledge to the flat rocks near the entrance to the cave.

"I know what the surprise is. A picnic dinner," declared Wealthy Richards with evident satisfaction, as she saw Mark approaching with a big covered basket, followed by Hallie with a steaming kettle.

"Oh, that's only the beginning of surprises," Ellen joyfully responded, opening the basket and taking out the pewter bowls and spoons, so when Hallie arrived they were all ready to be served. Mrs. Morley had brought a covered pan, which the others eyed with no little curiosity; and when they had finished the chowder she uncovered the wide dish and Ellen exclaimed: "Honey pudding!"

Made with corn meal, and containing all sorts of dried berries, and served with a sauce sweetened with honey, the Morley children all considered this pudding as one of the greatest of treats, and their guests all agreed with them.

Hallie gathered up the dishes and started off, and Faith said: "I am going to tell you about a secret that Ellen and I have kept for a whole year!"

"Ellen couldn't keep a secret a year," declared Mark.

"I could, Mark Morley; and I have," his sister instantly replied.

"I know! It's about 'Hero.' You never told us about him," said Letty.

"That's another secret," said Ellen. "We can't tell that 'til Father says we may. Now go on, Faith, and tell them about 'Verrazano.'"

And Faith told her story of discovering the cave; and of planning to take Ellen there a year ago; of their giving it the name of the early explorer of that coast, and calling each other by his name.

"We thought perhaps we could hide there against raiding parties, but we never have; and so now we are going to show it to you, and you can all have a share in it and come there whenever you want to," and Faith held back the boughs of the oak tree while the others, exclaiming over this real surprise, entered the cave. Nor did Ellen's father betray the fact that its existence had been known to him for many years.

Mark was perhaps the most surprised of any of the party. He wondered to himself how it had happened that his cousin instead of himself had found this cave, and he now thought "Verra" and "Zano" were not quite the silly names he had so often declared them.

Mr. Morley and Ellen led the way as they started back toward the house.

"Here is the first of your birthday gifts, daughter," he said as he handed her a bright silver shilling, over which she happily exclaimed.

"But this was to be a different birthday, Father. I was going to make presents instead of receiving them," she reminded him. Nevertheless Ellen promised herself that she would always keep the shilling; and when Hallie bestowed on her a string of blue beads, exactly like those she had given Faith, Ellen felt that after all gifts did make a birthday a more joyful occasion.

Hallie's box of beads had always been an enchanting mystery to the two girls. Where she obtained them she never revealed, but they were her chief treasure. There were beads of all sizes and colors, and both Faith and Ellen were well pleased to possess a necklace from Hallie's store.

Faith and the other girls reached the house in a few moments, and Ellen led the way to the sitting-room, where on the narrow table stood the three tiny thimble-boxes, which she now bestowed on her friends as a memento of her thirteenth birthday.

They all recalled the day when they had watched the destruction of Newport's Liberty Tree, and exclaimed over the clever workmanship of their gifts.

"Wealthy hasn't seen your puppets," Mary reminded Faith, and the two cousins were delighted to again set up the little figures and repeat the lines of "Victory" for Wealthy's benefit.

"When my next birthday comes we will have a party without a single British warship in Newport harbor," Ellen confidently declared as she bade her friends good-bye.

"It's more fun to give, presents than receive them," she said that night as she and Faith went upstairs to bed. "After this I am going to make gifts when my birthday comes."

"Well, each one of the girls left a little package for you, 'Verra.' They are in our room. Mary said not to tell you until they had gone."

"Oh!" exclaimed Ellen, flying up the stairs and running to the light-stand where lay a number of neatly wrapped packages.

"I'll open the littlest one first," she said, taking up one on which was written "From Wealthy to Ellen."

"Look, 'Zano'! Look!" and Ellen held up a tiny amber heart.

"Isn't it lovely! And just the thing to wear with Hallie's beads."

The next package was a fine handkerchief from Mary; and Letty's gift was a package of rock candy.

"Whatever can this be?" and Ellen held up a large package, and read aloud "From Faith and Mark."

"We made it together," Faith explained, as Ellen unwrapped a round covered basket made of sweet grass. "You can keep handkerchiefs in it "

"Only one more," said the excited Ellen, unrolling a soft bundle, "and this is from Mother! Whenever could she have made it without my knowing?" and she gazed admiringly at a short knitted jacket of pale blue, and instantly was out of the room running to find her mother to say how much she liked the gift.

"Well, it's nice to have birthdays," Ellen happily decided, as at a later hour than usual she and Faith prepared for bed.

"Do you suppose every new birthday will be better than the others, 'Zano'?"

"Maybe they will," Faith sleepily responded.

CHAPTER XIII

THE "GANSETT"

"We will have to help with the vegetable garden, 'Zano,'" Ellen informed her cousin one pleasant morning in mid-April, as the two girls were finishing their morning work of putting their room in order.

"It's harder than ever this year without Old Lion to do the plowing," she continued, and wondered why Faith gazed at her in such evident surprise.

"Come on; Mark wants us to plant squash seeds. He's waiting," and Ellen hurried her cousin through the house and across the yard to the edge of an open field.

"Here, Faith, take this basket and drop these seeds along this row," called Mark. "I'll keep right along with you and cover them up."

Faith carefully followed his directions. The springtime sunshine lay warmly over the garden; birds were singing in the apple trees that bordered the field, and everything seemed as peaceful as if England's fleet did not constantly menace the safety of Newport.

But Faith's thoughts were not on the pleasant quiet of the April morning; and as she worked on beside Mark she suddenly exclaimed:

147

"Mark, where is your boat? You haven't had it out this year."

"My boat is safe enough. I pulled it up under the brush near the cave. I mean to draw it down to the shore tonight. It will need caulking, and I mean to try and paint it before I put it afloat. But I'll have to do the work when I can find time. This garden has to be planted or we won't have much to eat when fall comes," Mark responded.

"I'll help, Mark, with the boat. Couldn't I?" Faith asked eagerly.

"All right, if you want to. We might begin tonight," agreed Mark.

"I'll help, too," called Ellen from the next row, where she was at work with her father; and the three cousins now looked forward to the end of the day when they could begin to set Mark's boat once more into the peaceful waters of the cove; and Mark promised the girls that they should go with him on his first fishing excursion.

At noon Mr. Morley told the girls he would not need their help for the remainder of the day; and Mark found time in the late afternoon to go with them to the cove and draw out his boat from the underbrush where it had been securely covered, and they all set to work brushing and cleaning the little craft.

Mark pointed out where its seams needed caulking, and by sunset they had already made a good start on the necessary repairs, and in a few days the "Gansett," as Mark named his boat, had received a good coat of blue paint and was ready to slide into the water.

"I'll use those fine oars you girls got ashore when you sank the raiders' boat," said Mark, on a morning in early May when they were ready to set forth on their first cruise.

Mark again wore his "pirate's cap" of blue cotton twisted about his head, and Faith and Ellen were bareheaded, their yellow hair tightly braided, and they wore the faded blue flannel dresses that had already done them good service.

As Mark pushed the boat clear from the shore "Hero," with a triumphant bark, came racing across the sand and sprang on board.

"Let's take him, Mark," pleaded Ellen; and, as the spaniel settled meekly down beside the girls, Mark made no objection, and the "Gansett" was soon beyond the ledges and headed toward one of the small islands, near which Mark meant to fish.

"Mark, I'll wager you don't dare go within hailing distance of that ship," said Ellen, pointing toward a tall-masted cruiser that swung quietly at anchor.

"Why not?" Mark instantly responded, as he changed the direction of his boat so that the "Gansett" was now headed directly toward the warship, and at the same moment "Hero" jumped to the side of the boat and began barking loudly.

As the dog leaped he struck against one of the oars, sending it out of Mark's grasp. Before he could recover it the oar was out of reach. Nor would "Hero" be silent; his excited yelps echoed across the calm waters, and Faith looking anxiously toward the ship could see that a number of sailors were leaning over the rail evidently watching the commotion on board the rowboat, which now in the current of the tide was being swept nearer and nearer to the enemy's ship.

"Hero's" excitement increased; he appeared eager to jump from the boat and swim toward the vessel, and kept up a series of joyful barks as if sure of his welcome, so that Faith and Ellen clutched him firmly, and did not pay much attention to Mark's efforts to keep the "Gansett" clear of the ship.

Not until they heard a voice calling, "That's 'Jimpsey.' That's my dog," did they realize what was happening: that this was undoubtedly the very ship from which the raiding party of a year ago had set forth, and into whose boat they had pushed the boulder; and that now "Hero's" master recognized the dog and would surely take possession of it.

"Oh, Mark! Whatever can we do?" wailed Faith.

But Mark made no response. The "Gansett" was now very near the cruiser's side. He could plainly see the faces of the men leaning over the rail, could hear their laughter, and see that a man was half over the rail calling: "Jump, 'Jimpsey'! Come on!" to the now half-frantic "Hero," who sprang from the girl's clutching hands and reached the ship's deck, amid the cheers of the delighted sailors.

Then came a sharp word of command, and a seaman quickly lowered himself into the "Gansett."

"Up with you," he said gruffly, grasping Mark's shoulder, and pushing him toward the rope that swung from the railing.

But Mark firmly resisted. "I'm not going to leave my boat," he declared.

"Oh, yes you are. And these little maids will follow you," responded the sailor, with a not unkindly glance at the two frightened girls. "I'll see they get up safely and that no harm befalls them," he added, and at this Mark grasped the swinging rope and was drawn safely on board; and, aided by their captor, Faith and Ellen followed him.

"The American Navy," laughed a young officer, as the three adventurers reached the deck, where "Hero" seemed perfectly at home.

"Where did you get this dog?" questioned the man who had called "Jimpsey."

"Found him on the ledges half-drowned, nearly a year ago," Mark answered.

"Well, you have taken good care of him, and I'm obliged to you," the man responded. "Lost an oar, didn't you? Where were you bound?"

"Fishing," Mark briefly replied.

"And these little maids are your crew? Now that you are on board his Majesty's ship don't you want to look about a bit?" he continued, smiling at the girls.

"No, thank you," Faith managed to reply, while Ellen shook her head, her reproachful glance fixed on the ungrateful "Hero."

"Give the boy an oar and start them off," said the smiling officer. "I'm sure 'Jimpsey' is worth the price of an oar."

But Faith was resolved to at least make some effort to take "Hero" with them.

"'Hero! Hero!'" she called; and the spaniel cocked his head and wagged his tail as if well pleased by her notice, but kept close beside his former owner.

"You can't make an American rebel out of 'Jimpsey,'" the man laughingly declared. "Tell me where you live, and I'll bring him to see you sometime," he added; but Mark clasped her arm saying:

"The sailor is waiting to lower you into the boat," and drew her toward the rail, with Ellen holding fast to her cousin's arm, and in a few moments they were again in the little rowboat, and the promised oar handed down to Mark; and again the sailors gathered at the rail smiling down at them.

As Mark pushed off from the ship's side the men cheered the tiny craft, and "Hero's" joyful bark echoed in their ears.

They were all silent until there was a wide space

of blue water between the "Gansett" and the English vessel. Then Ellen tearfully exclaimed: "It's all my fault. I dared Mark to go near that cruiser, so of course he would. And now they have taken 'Hero'! Oh, dear! I don't know what Hallie will say."

"It's their dog, anyway," Mark responded.

"I wouldn't have believed 'Hero' would leave us for anybody," said Faith; and to this Mark made no answer. He was thinking angrily of his own clumsiness in losing the oar, and he had a certain admiration and approval for the spaniel's faithful affection for its first owner.

The fishing excursion ended earlier than they had planned; for the girls could think and talk only of the morning's adventure, and mourn over the loss of "Hero"; and as soon as Mark had secured a number of good-sized cod he headed the "Gansett" for home, taking care to keep a good distance from the fleet.

Hallie listened to Ellen's story of their adventure with many angry exclamations.

"Taking that innercent little dog! They takes everything. Our horse gone, and now our dog," she mourned; and when Mark reminded her that "Hero" belonged to the sailor who claimed him, she was more wrathful than ever.

"His real name is 'Jimpsey,'" said Faith.

"'Jimpsey! Jimpsey'?" repeated Hallie, and began to chuckle and laugh as if she had entirely forgotten the loss of the spaniel; from time to time during the remainder of the day the girls heard her repeating "Jimpsey," as if finding satisfaction in the queer name.

"It's just as if 'Hero' made us a visit," Faith said a few days after their adventure, as she and Ellen started down the lane on their way to Newport for an afternoon visit with Wealthy Richards.

"Do you suppose we will ever see him again?" Ellen mournfully responded.

"Maybe we will. Maybe they will bring him on shore some day and he will find his way back to us," Faith hopefully declared; but Ellen had little belief that they would ever see "Hero" again.

As they entered the town and made their way toward the Richards' house the girls noticed that the streets seemed unusually full of red-coated soldiers. Boats were plying between the fleet and the wharves, and there was an air of evident excitement.

"Perhaps the British are going away," said Ellen; but the moment they greeted Wealthy her first words destroyed the hope of such a possibility.

"Oh, girls! I'm so glad to see you. And whatever do you think of this! The British are expecting more troops. And they have sent six hundred men to attack Bristol and Warren, and destroy the American boats in the Kickemuit River. Father says General Sullivan has only sixteen hundred men, and that he knows not what may befall us unless Washington sends us aid."

"Well, where are those French vessels that were coming to help us?" demanded Faith, as Wealthy led them into a pleasant room whose windows looked out on a garden behind the house.

"Take off your sunbonnets, and I'll bring you a cool drink," said Wealthy, and Faith and Ellen were glad to rest after their long walk; and when Wealthy appeared bringing a round copper tray with mugs filled with raspberry shrub, and a plate of crisp molasses cookies, they forgot all about the dangers that threatened the town, and smiled happily as Wealthy told them that Mary and Letty had promised to come and share their visit.

"I have a fine swing in the garden," Wealthy continued, "and we will go out there when they come."

"Oh, Wealthy! We've lost 'Hero.' And we have been aboard a British warship. Yes, we truly have! And 'Hero's' real name is 'Jimpsey,'" said Ellen; and, in response to Wealthy's wondering questions, she told the story of the adventure that had ended in the loss of the brown spaniel.

"But he will come back, Ellen. I'm sure he will," said Wealthy. "Perhaps he is in Newport this very day. Boats have been coming from the ships all the morning."

But Ellen shook her head mournfully.

"He doesn't want to come back. He was ready to jump overboard and swim to the ship if Faith and I hadn't held on to him."

"Here's Mary and Letty," exclaimed Faith, and then the story of "Hero's" loss had to be retold as Wealthy led the way to the garden and to the swing suspended from the stout bough of a big oak tree.

The afternoon passed happily, and the girls enjoyed eating their supper in the garden; and an hour before sunset bade their friends good-bye and started for home. As they left Thames Street a body of mounted horsemen with jingling spurs and bridle reins rode past them, and Ellen excitedly exclaimed:

"Old Lion! 'Verra,' did you see him? It was our horse," but the little troop was so quickly out of sight that neither of the girls could be sure that the grey horse was really their own valued Old Lion; and they hurried on, eager to escape from the unusual noise and confusion of the town.

It did not occur to either of them that if rumors of the coming of the French had reached the Americans their British foes had even more accurate information; and General Pigot was already strengthening his forces at Butt's Hill, in case of a sudden attack by General Sullivan, and sending re-enforcements to various points.

In a short time the cousins had left Newport behind them when suddenly a familiar bark made them quickly turn to gaze back along the road, and to discover racing toward them an excited brown spaniel whose feet seemed hardly to touch the ground as he bounded along.

"Oh, It's 'Hero'! It's 'Hero'!" exclaimed Ellen. "It truly is!"

"'Jimpsey! Jimpsey'!" echoed the delighted Faith, and they ran to meet the little dog that they had not dared hope ever again to behold.

CHAPTER XIV

THE FLAGS OF FRANCE

"'Jimpsey'!" exclaimed Hallie, as the spaniel leaped happily about her. "You 'scaped quick as you could, didn't you, 'Jimpsey,'" and henceforth she delighted in calling him by this name; and he seemed ready to answer to either "Hero" or "Jimpsey," and well pleased to be once more the center of interest in the Morley household.

"He'd be off like a flash if he caught sight of that sailor," said Mark; but Faith and Ellen promptly disputed this statement.

"He wanted to come back to us; of course he did, Mark; and just as soon as he got on shore he started to find his way home," she said, and "Jimpsey" gave a sharp bark as if to confirm her words.

"You'd better not take him to Newport just the same, or let him go yelping along the shore or he'll be aboard that ship again," Mark persisted, and the girls agreed that it would be wise not to give the dog his former freedom.

It was undoubtedly a fortunate impulse that brought the spaniel back to the Morley farm; and perhaps even his former owner would have rejoiced in knowing of

"Jimpsey's" safety if he could have known the dangers that were now, in June 1778, so rapidly encircling the British ships in Newport harbor.

The three American seaports held by the British at this time were New York, Philadelphia, and Newport. In early July Philadelphia was once more under American control; so only Never York and Newport remained for D'Estaing to choose between as objects of attack when the French fleet should really appear; and, as approach to New York was a difficult matter because of the draught of the French vessels, D'Estaing decided upon attacking the British at Newport.

Faith and Ellen continued to make frequent visits to the cave, but "Hero" was no longer permitted to accompany them. Climbing the ledge the girls would gaze anxiously toward the tall-masted ships fearing lest they should see a boat set out toward their shore. But June passed without any new movement on the part of the British. "Hero," apparently well content, followed Mark about the fields and accepted Hallie's constant approval as if he had well earned it.

Berries were again ripening along the pasture slopes, and one day in late July Faith and Ellen set forth for the ravine near the Overing house, where Faith had witnessed the capture of the British General Prescott.

But today there was no plan for a clambake on the shore. They meant to fill their baskets with raspberries as quickly as possible, and return home in time for the midday meal. They kept close together, and Faith again told the story of her night in the ravine, and of seeing the "bundle" that Major Barton's men were hurrying toward the shore; and Ellen recalled the fishing excursion when Mark had encountered the soldiers who were searching for the deserter.

"It was mean of them to take our luncheon, and Mark's flint and steel," said Ellen.

And now Faith decided to tell her cousin of her own part in the deserter's fortunate escape:

"Listen, Ellen. It wasn't the redcoats who took those things. I took them! Yes, I did. The flint and steel, and the food. When I was gathering the seaweed I found the man who was trying to escape the soldiers, and I gave the things to him," and Faith quickly told the story of securing the food from Hallie's pantry, of taking Mark's boots, and the articles front the trunk in the attic, and carrying them to the injured man hiding among the rocks.

"And he told me I was his only friend in America," she concluded, as Ellen, nearly speechless with amazement, gazed at her cousin as if she could hardly believe in the possibility of such an adventure.

"And you never told me, all this time, Faith! Why didn't you?"

"I wanted to, Ellen. But the man made me promise not to tell anyone. But now it's so long ago it can't matter. I meant for him to go to our secret cave and stay there until he was stronger, but he didn't wait for me," Faith somewhat mournfully responded.

"Faith, I believe that man was the very one who got to the American camp at Tiverton and told Major Barton about Prescott's visiting that house," said Ellen, with a nod in the direction of the Overing place, "and if he did then you are the one who ought to have the credit for capturing him," declared the excited Ellen, nearly upsetting her half filled basket as she jumped to her feet.

"You probably saved his life," she added, "and if ever the British leave Newport I'll wager that deserter comes back to thank you. Are you going to let me tell Mark? "

Faith shook her head. "I guess we'd better keep it a secret a while longer, 'Verra,'" she soberly responded; and to this Ellen reluctantly agreed. But on their way home she urged Faith to tell the story to Mark and her father and mother.

"No one else need ever know about it, 'Zano,'" she urged, "and Mark has always hated to think that one of those soldiers has his flint and steel. They would all be glad you helped that man."

And at last Faith consented. "It can't do Hugh Ramsay any harm if nobody else knows," she said; and Ellen now hurried her cousin across fields and pastureland eager to reach home and see the surprise of the family when Faith told the adventurous tale.

But Mark met them with news which for the moment made the girls completely forget their own story.

On the previous evening, from the ledge near the cave, the girls had watched a sloop of war, under the British flag, and it sailed into the harbor and anchored near the fleet; but Mark had been the only one to attach much importance to this arrival.

"It's to bring General Pigot news of the French fleet, I'll wager it is," he had declared; and when the girls started off after berries Mark was already on his way to Newport, hoping to gather news about the sloop. He was just home, and came running to meet them.

"That sloop is the 'Falcon,'" he announced, "and everybody in Newport knows that it brought messages from Admiral Lord Howe and General Clinton to tell General Pigot and Commodore Brisbane that the French fleet are off Sandy Hook, and sailing in this direction. They may come in sight any time. You ought to see how excited the British are. Pigot is getting ready for a battle. I hope General Sullivan is ready," and the excited boy sped off toward the house to tell the great news to his father and mother.

Ellen and Faith hurried after him. "If we go down to the ledge we can watch for the first sight of the French vessels," Ellen said, as they carried the berries into the kitchen. But Mrs. Morley shook her head at this suggestion.

"They may fire at once on the British ships, and you are safer at home," she said, so the girls contented themselves by peering from the upper windows, and wondering if Mark's news was really true.

Before it was quite light the next morning, July 27th, 1778, all Newport was astir and on the outlook for the French vessels. The British were showing hurried preparations for defense; and the American citizens were hopeful that some way might now be found to clear Newport and its harbor of their foes.

The Morleys were just finishing their early breakfast when Faith, happening to glance out of a window, sprang up from her chair and ran toward the open door exclaiming:

"Here come the girls!" and Ellen was quickly after her, and they ran down the slope to meet Wealthy, Letty, and Mary who were hurrying toward them, and Letty called out:

"A fleet of vessels has been seen toward the southeast. It's steering straight toward the island, and nobody knows whether they are the French or more British ships."

"Everybody in Newport is afraid the town will be fired on," panted Wealthy.

"And our mothers said we could stay out here all day," added Mary, as the astonished cousins welcomed these unexpected visitors.

Mr. and Mrs. Morley and Mark were now all at the

door, and questioned Mary as to what they had heard of a possible attack on the town.

"'Tis said General Sullivan has re-enforcements from the other American colonies, and his troops are in Providence; and that they may already be moving toward Newport," she said, as "Jimpsey" came leaping to welcome the newcomers; and for a moment the girls forgot all their excitement over the possibilities of an encounter between the American and British forces in their surprise at seeing the spaniel, and listened eagerly as Ellen told the story of his return.

"I guess he escaped just in time. If those ships are the French fleet they'll sink the British vessels before they can escape," declared Mark.

"Can't we all go down on the ledges and watch for the first sight of them?" asked Wealthy; and, when Mrs. Morley had been convinced that no immediate danger would be incurred, and when "Jimpsey" had been shut indoors, Mark and the girls started off for the shore.

The July morning was warm and clear; gulls hovered over the sandy cove, and everything seemed as peaceful and quiet as usual as the little group made its way along the shore and climbed the ledge to the flat rocks near the oak tree.

"No one can see us here," said Faith, as they stood gazing toward the British ships.

"And we can hide in the cave if we want to," Ellen added.

"That sloop is hoisting her sails; it's going out to reconnoitre," declared Mark, as a sloop-of-war left the fleet and headed toward the mouth of the harbor.

They were all silent as they watched the swift-sailing craft put out to sea; perhaps it was going to welcome British cruisers, whose coming would mean more trouble for the Americans; but Faith and Mark were confident that before the day ended they would welcome D'Estaing's ships.

"There they are. Look! Look!" Mark exclaimed, jumping to his feet and pointing seaward.

"Oh! Count them, Faith!" said Ellen, her glance fixed on the stately warships of France that now appeared at the entrance of the harbor.

"Sixteen! Sixteen!" Faith and Mary shouted, just as a cannon shot from the sloop of war sounded across the bay.

It remained unanswered, nor did the two following salutes receive any response from the French vessels.

"That settles it. It's the French," said Mark. And now they intently watched the distant squadron as it steadily approached; and as it came to anchor at the entrance of Newport harbor all at once the white flag with the Three Lilies sprang out at every masthead.

"Hurrah!" shouted Mark leaping about the ledge. "Now we'll see what the British will do when General Sullivan attacks them by land, and the French by sea. 'Tis the end of the British."

But this hopeful prediction was not to be fulfilled until long after this appearance of the French fleet, whose ships now completely blocked the entrance to Newport harbor, twelve warships and four frigates.

For a time the little group on the ledge stood gazing toward the fleets. They had expected that the French would at once fire upon the enemy; but they lay quietly at anchor, and Mark was now eager to be off to Newport to discover, if possible, if Pigot's men were ready for battle.

"Father won't let you go, Mark," Ellen confidently asserted. "Didn't you hear what Mary said—that Pigot's soldiers were driving everybody off Newport's street?"

Mark made no reply. His thoughts were so intent on the probable movements of General Sullivan's troops that he almost forgot his companions as he ran swiftly toward home.

"You can see the girls safely to their homes when their visit is over," Mr. Morley agreed; so Mark made the most of the intervening time by returning to the shore and endeavoring to discover if there was any movement among the British ships.

That afternoon the girls could talk of nothing but the beautiful white flags with their blue lilies that floated above the French fleet, and of the speedy departure of the English.

"Mary, sing us that song that your father taught

you," urged Letty, as the girls seated themselves in the shade of the elm tree near the kitchen door, "the one American soldiers sang after the British were driven out of Boston."

"The one that begins 'Sons of Valor'?" asked Mary.

"Yes, I know part of it," Letty replied.

"So do I," added Wealthy.

Mary smiled, and began the song, in which Letty and Wealthy quickly joined:

"Sons of valor, taste the glories
of your rightful liberty,
Sing a triumph o'er the Tories,
Let the pulse of hope beat high.

If their fleet at fair Rhode Island
Dare to combat with the brave,
Driven from each dale and highland,
They shall plough the distant wave.

War, fierce war shall break their forces,
Nerves of Tory men shall fail
Seeing Howe, with altered courses,
Bending to the blasting gale."

"Oh, girls, that song is as good for Newport as it was for Boston," said Faith, and before the others could speak, Letty, to a gay dancing tune, sang:

"Now let us praise America
　And France in union with her;
　Sadly shall Britain rue the day
　Her hostile fleet came hither."

Mr. and Mrs. Morley were standing in the doorway, and Hallie smiled from an open window, and as Letty finished Mr. Morley said:

"I hope your songs prove a true prophecy, girls. And with the French to help us perhaps they will."

Mary now declared they must start for home, and Mark could hardly conceal his impatience to be off. Faith and Ellen walked down the lane with their guests; and as they said good-bye Faith soberly remarked:

"We'll all remember, all our lives, maybe, that we saw the French fleet sail into Newport harbor."

"And the flags, Faith, the white flags with their three lilies," Wealthy added.

"Yes, the flags of France," responded Faith.

CHAPTER XV

A SEPTEMBER'S ADVENTURE

In the days following the arrival of the French fleet in Newport harbor Faith and Ellen were kept closely at home, for no one could foresee where battles might occur. From the upper chambers of the Morley house, in the early days of August 1778, they excitedly watched the destruction of British armed vessels, destroyed by the orders of the commodore of the fleet, that they might not be captured by the Americans.

It was on August the eighth that D'Estaing entered the harbor, and found it an easy matter to clear the bay of the remaining British ships. By General Pigot's orders Newport was now entirely closed; no one except British soldiers was to enter or leave the town; the heavy cannonade from the French fleet and the return fire from the British batteries echoed along fields and shore.

The Marquis de Lafayette had come to the aid of General Sullivan with two thousand men; and assaulted by the American forces on land and by the French fleet at sea there was hope that the British were completely trapped.

But before this could be accomplished a British

fleet of thirteen ships and seven frigates, under the command of Admiral Lord Howe, came in sight off Point Judith, and D'Estaing put to sea to give them battle.

As the days passed and the French fleet did not return, having encountered a violent tempest, which damaged both fleets more than their battle against each other, and obliged D'Estaing to sail to Boston for repairs, General Sullivan found it necessary to retreat. He was promptly pursued by General Pigot, and the "Battle of Rhode Island" followed.

Overwhelmed by the large forces of the British the Americans retreated; and now the people of Newport were again left to the mercy of the British invaders. The "Lilies of France" on the French flags, that had seemed to promise good fortune and success, as the group of girls on the ledge had delightedly watched the arrival of D'Estaing's ships, had brought only disappointment; and Newport was now to face even greater hardships than she had yet known.

There were no more visits from their friends in Newport for the two cousins, and Mark could no longer enter the town and bring home tidings of possible freedom. The girls helped gather the small harvest from the garden, mended their worn clothing, and stayed more closely at home than ever before.

"Just think, 'Zano'; we thought by this time that American ships would bring all sorts of things to

Newport, and that we would have new dresses," Ellen mournfully announced one September morning, as she held up a faded gingham dress, so worn that it seemed hardly possible it could do further service.

"And Mark and father's clothes are dreadful," she continued. "Mark hasn't a decent shirt. They are as badly off for things to wear as that deserter you found hiding among the ledges."

Faith with a quick exclamation of "Trunks," at which the surprised Ellen could only wonder, had darted from the room in search of her aunt. She had suddenly remembered the trunks in the attic from which she had taken clothing for the deserter, and recalled that her aunt had told her that their contents were her own.

"She said I could do whatever I liked with the things when 'the right time came.' Oh! I ought to have remembered. This is surely the right time, when Uncle Morley and Mark need things," she reproachfully told herself as she found her aunt in the kitchen.

"Aunt Cynthia! Those trunks in the attic! You said I could do what I liked with the things. And there are shirts and coats. I know, because I opened one and got clothes for the man, Hugh Ramsay, the one the soldiers were after, and—" but Faith's excited story was interrupted by her aunt's surprised exclamation:

"Whatever are you talking about, child? Who is Hugh Ramsay?" and Mrs. Morley gazed at her niece as if wondering if she knew what she was saying.

"I know, Mother!" said Ellen, who came running into the kitchen. "Faith helped a deserter to escape. Tell about it, Faith!"

"Yes, I did help him. I gave him Mark's flint and steel, and food from Hallie's pantry, and—"

"And my boots, I'll wager that's what became of them," said Mark who had just entered the room; and with exclamations from the amazed Hallie, and approving words from Mark, Faith told the story of that March day when she had discovered the fleeing British soldier and brought him food and clothing.

"Let's go up to the attic and open the trunks," she concluded; and leading the way Faith was running up the stairs before her aunt could say a word.

The others followed her, and as Faith opened the trunk and began to take out the shirts, coats, stockings and other clothing, Mark's face brightened, for he had more than once wondered where his father and he could obtain clothing.

"What's in this trunk?" Faith asked, turning to a long leather-covered trunk which stood near the one she had just emptied.

"Your mother's dresses, dear child," replied her aunt, thinking how she had hoped not to open this trunk until Faith was really grown up.

"Then there will be things for us," said Ellen, looking down at her well mended skirt.

As Faith promptly lifted the cover she exclaimed:

"A shawl, Aunt Cynthia, just what you need," and drew out a brown shawl with deep fringes.

"Didn't Mother have pretty things?" she continued admiringly, as she took out a full-skirted gown of soft brown wool, trimmed with braid, and a long coat of a darker shade.

There was a dress of lilac silk patterned with tiny pale green wreaths; a skirt of blue plaided wool; a cape of deep blue broadcloth; and a quantity of underwear, as well as other dresses; and as the girls looked at all these riches they exchanged a delighted smile, and looked forward to the dresses they would soon possess.

And indeed the clothing would prove a godsend to all the family. Faith was right in deciding that it was "the right time" to make use of it. It gave them all new courage, and Mrs. Morley and the girls were busy all that morning sorting out the garments that could at once be used, and others that could be made over for Faith and Ellen. The lilac silk gown, however, was carefully wrapped and put back in the trunk, together with a dainty lace parasol, gloves and slippers.

"You must keep these, Faith, for some great occasion," Mrs. Morley said, and Faith soberly agreed, wondering to herself if there would ever come a time when she would wear anything but the plainest garments.

Mark, rejoicing in the possession of new shirts, stockings, and a good supply of handkerchiefs, and the speedy prospect of new trousers and jacket, as soon as his mother could remodel the garments, was more hopeful than he had been for weeks; and Mr. Morley was glad again to be decently clothed.

The days that followed were busy days for the two cousins. Seated beneath the big elm tree they carefully ripped the seams of the coats and trousers which were to be made over for Mark, and then carried the garments to the kitchen for Hallie to sponge and press them. Then Mrs. Morley would cut them to the proper size for Mark.

"Our turn will come next," Ellen hopefully declared, as they completed this task, "and Mother says we can both have dresses from that brown wool, and jackets from the big blue cape. And all because you helped the deserter, 'Zano.' It's just like a wonderful present, isn't it?"

Faith nodded her assent; but, glad as she was that the trunks had furnished clothing for all the family, she owned to herself that she was tired of ripping long seams; and the prospect of now beginning the same task on dresses, and then helping to make them into gowns for Ellen and herself seemed to her a long undertaking, and when Mark suggested that they should go for a trip in the "Gansett" that afternoon she eagerly hoped her aunt would give them permission.

After many cautionings, Mrs. Morley agreed, and the three cousins set out for the shore, with "Hero's" complaining barks echoing in their ears.

The September afternoon was warm and clear, the sun glinted on the smooth waters of the harbor, and when Mark gave his consent for Faith to row one of the oars she felt sure that the world was a very pleasant place, and Newport harbor, despite Admiral Howe's warships, the best of all.

Ellen, perched in the bow of the boat, sang to herself as their little craft left the cove, and headed toward the island that lay a mile from shore. As Ellen sang the same words over and over:

> "King George and all his wicked laws,
>   His guns and warships too,
>   We do deny and here defy,
>   And he his acts shall rue,"

Mark and Faith at last joined in the song, and their voices clearly sounded across the distance that lay between them and a British frigate. But the sailors took no notice of the little craft as the "Gansett" sped on toward the fishing grounds; and, carefully selecting a place not far from shore, Mark anchored the boat, drew in the oars, and provided the girls with fishing lines and well-baited hooks.

They were all quiet, attending strictly to their purpose of catching as many fish as possible; and in a short time the box that Mark always brought on such excursions was well filled, and he declared they had enough.

"If we catch any more we'd have to put them in the bottom of the boat, and I don't want the 'Gansett' all messed up," he said, winding up his lines, and preparing to pull up the anchor.

"There's lots of blackberries on that island. We used to come berrying there; this is just the time they are ripe," said Ellen, gazing toward the wooded shore of the little island.

"We haven't any basket," Mark reminded her.

"We could twist up some sort of a basket with leaves and grass," Faith said, "and it's too early to go, home. Let's go ashore, Mark."

"All right, maybe that's a good plan. Mother and Hallie will be glad enough for the berries," he replied; and headed the boat toward a tiny cove between the ledges.

A strong pull on the oars sent the boat well up on the sandy beach, and Ellen and Faith ran to the rough clearing in search of the broad plantain leaves, from which they would make a sort of basket to hold the berries; Mark quickly followed them, and they were soon busy pinning the leaves together with green twigs, and twisting long grass about them for greater security.

As Ellen had said, the blackberries were plenty. Dead ripe they hung black and juicy from the prickly vines, and their leaf baskets were quickly filled and carried to the boat.

"Put them well up in the bow, and cover them with more leaves," suggested Mark, and this was done. Then more baskets were made; and, jubilant over this unexpected addition to the food supplies they would carry home, the cousins talked happily of their successful excursion, and of what Hallie would say when they brought the blackberries to her kitchen.

Intent on filling their baskets they had now wandered some distance from the shore; and they did not notice the dark clouds gathering in the western sky, or the little threatening whiffs of wind that bent the treetops. Not until a distant rumbling of thunder made Faith exclaim, "Is that guns?" and Mark responded, "It's thunder! Look at the sky!" and darted off through the underbrush toward the shore to make sure that his boat was safe, did the girls realize that the storm was already upon them.

Sheltering themselves as much as possible by crawling under the low growing branches of a group of spruce trees, the two girls listened to the reverberating peals of thunder that echoed over the harbor. The rain came down in torrents, and the wind bent the slender trees as it swept across the little island.

"Oh, 'Zano,' I'm afraid Mark will be swept into the sea," said Ellen.

"Of course he won't," Faith resolutely assured her; "and if he is he can swim."

But Ellen was not so easily comforted. As the rain continued and the force of the wind increased she became more and more alarmed for her brother's safety.

"Maybe he got into the boat and it has been swept out into the harbor," she moaned, as she crept closer in among the branches that sheltered them.

CHAPTER XVI

A DANGEROUS CRUISE

Pushing his way through the underbrush with the rain dashing against his face, Mark hurried on toward the shore hoping the little "Gansett" was too securely fastened to be swept away by the strong wind. At times he could hardly be sure of his way because of boughs striking against his face, and the sudden darkness of the storm.

But at last he came out at the rough clearing, and peered anxiously down at the little cove.

"She's gone!" he muttered, running to the shore, where now the waves were dashing far up the beach.

There was nothing he could do; but he ran along the shore with the vain hope of discovering the boat lodged against the outstanding ledges.

Thoroughly drenched by the downpour Mark now paid little attention to the storm as he climbed over rocks and crawled along the wet ledge that ran out into the harbor. But no sight of the "Gansett" rewarded his search; and at last he turned to make his way back to where he had left Faith and Ellen crouching for shelter under the wide branches of the spruce trees.

"If we call maybe that will help Mark find us," Faith

suggested, as they began listening eagerly for sounds that might tell of his return; and instantly Ellen shouted his name; and they continued to call until they heard his voice in response, and he came crashing through the bushes to crawl in beside them.

"The boat's gone," he briefly announced; "not a sight of her. Maybe dashed into kindling wood by this time."

"Oh, Mark! And our fine berries all lost," wailed Ellen.

"Berries," Mark scornfully echoed. "What's berries? The 'Gansett' is worth all the berries in the world."

"Maybe the boat isn't lost, Mark. Maybe when it clears we'll find her safely ashore," Faith hopefully suggested.

The wind died away soon after Mark's return; the rain ceased, and the brief tempest ended in a glorious sunset. As the cousins crawled out from under the sheltering boughs they at once hurried toward the shore, too anxious about the fate of the boat to pay much attention to each other's well soaked garments.

Mark led the way, and the girls followed him into a rough clearing that sloped to a sandy cove.

"There, you can see for yourself, no sign of the 'Gansett,'" he soberly declared.

"Whatever can we do, Mark? We'll never get home. Father hasn't any boat to come after us, and we've nothing to eat," sobbed Ellen.

It did indeed seem a perilous situation for the cousins. The sun was already sinking below the western horizon, and the chill of the September evening would soon make them conscious of their damp clothing. The little island offered no place of shelter, or means of securing any food beyond such berries as they might find; nor could they hope for any speedy rescue.

As Ellen declared, her father could not start in search of them, for the "Gansett" was their only boat.

"I've a mind to try and make the sailors on that British frigate come after us and take us home. If we all go out on that ledge and wave and shout they would surely see us," said Mark.

"They wouldn't come," Ellen dolefully responded, "and if they did they might just set us ashore a long way from home. And, anyway, I'd rather stay here all night than ask them."

"We may have to stay here more than one night. We'd better look about while it is light and make us some sort of a shelter," replied Mark, and nothing more was said of asking aid from the enemy; and they ran along the clearing hoping to find a place where they could find some degree of comfort for the night.

Faith, while her cousins talked, had been gazing about the cove. It seemed larger than the one where they had landed, and where was the overhanging oak tree that she had noticed? Surely the sudden tempest had not swept it away!

"It isn't the same cove," she told herself, running along the little stretch of sandy beach, and climbing the ledge beyond.

"What is Faith doing?" exclaimed Ellen, her attention suddenly attracted by a loud shout from her cousin as Faith waved her arms and jumped about as if she had encountered a sea serpent.

"She can't be trying to signal the British frigate, can she, Mark? Oh! She's gone over the ledge!" and with a shriek of terror Ellen ran swiftly toward the shore with Mark quickly darting past her. They both feared that their cousin had slipped on the wet rocks, and that she was now struggling in the deep water.

Reaching the summit of the ledge from which Faith had so suddenly disappeared, Mark and Ellen gazed down in speechless astonishment at the scene below. There lay a tiny sandy cove, over which hung the wide branches of a sturdy oak; and there swinging safely in the calm waters was a blue boat, their own "Gansett"; while Faith was pulling vigorously on the rope that held it to the shore.

"It's got to be bailed out, Mark," she called, as her cousins came hurrying toward her. "It's half full of water; but I don't believe it touched the berries. They were so far up in the bow and so well covered."

"Berries! What's berries!" Mark scornfully responded, as with a strong pull on the rope he brought the boat within reach and drew it well up on the shore;

and speedily discovered that oars, fish, and berries were safe.

It was no wonder that Mark had lost his bearings in the blinding wind and rain, and mistaken the larger cove for the one where he had left the "Gansett" safely moored. Beyond their fear of being held on the island, no harm had resulted from his mistake; and they all set vigorously to work bailing the water from the little craft, eager to start for home before darkness should cover the harbor and make it difficult for them to steer their course.

Mark was quite ready for Faith to help row; and as they pulled out from the sheltering cove they were all in the best of spirits, thinking themselves fortunate indeed to escape from the island. Ellen was eager to give Faith all the credit for finding the "Gansett."

"It's always Faith who finds ways to do things," she said, as she again established herself comfortably in the bow.

"Keep a good outlook, Ellen. The tide is setting out, and it will be dark by the time we pass the frigate. I don't want to get too near it," Mark said, as the "Gansett" passed out beyond the ledges and headed across the harbor.

Although the sun had set in a clear sky, dark clouds hovered along the eastern horizon. Twilight was deepening into darkness, and with the tide against them it was no easy matter to keep the little boat headed toward home. Faith's arms began to ache from the steady pull on the oar, and her hands burned uncomfortably as she tightened her grip.

"Lights, Mark! Oh, we are close to a ship," called Ellen, in so shrill a voice that her companions instantly ceased rowing, and a moment later the bow of the "Gansett" swung against a stout anchor chain.

"Push off, Faith!" whispered Mark, and as Faith thrust her oar against the massive iron links that held the British frigate securely at anchor, it flashed through her mind how she had once believed such chains could easily be filed through and so set the enemy ships adrift.

"I'll never think that again," she told herself. "'Twould take a week to file through one link."

But there was no time for her to let her thoughts wander; for there came sharp calls from the high deck of the frigate; lights flashed over its bow; and the glimmer along gun barrels gave the cousins an instant sense of their danger, as they gazed up at the dark bulk that towered above them.

Lanterns now swung over the ship's side, and the faces of a group of sailors peered down at them, as a gruff voice demanded:

"What boat is that? What do you want?"

"We want to go home," wailed Ellen. "We got caught in the storm."

"Make sure there's not a boarding fleet using those children as a decoy," came a command; for the British in Newport in the autumn of 1778 were not taking any possible chance of being defeated by Yankee cleverness. They knew that General Sullivan's army had been strongly re-enforced, and they still feared the possible return of D'Estaing's ships, that still lingered at Boston; and this sudden appearance of a boat, even if its crew consisted only of two girls and a half-grown boy, was not to be disregarded.

A sailor swung himself down by a stout rope, and flashed a lantern over the "Gansett." Mark answered his questions; and the man, evidently amused at the sight of the bedraggled little group, was drawn back to the frigate's deck as he called:

"No danger from this craft," and bidding Mark push off, and to learn better than to run afoul of the biggest ship in the harbor, he disappeared over the rail.

Mark and Faith put forth all their strength as they bent to their oars, and again headed the "Gansett" toward home.

"I was sure they'd take our berries and fish," whimpered Ellen.

They were all silent the greater part of the way. Not until Ellen called out that she could see a light moving along the dark line of the shore, and Mark declared that it must be their father searching for some sign of them, did they feel any sense of safety. And when in response to Mark's hail of: "Here's the 'Gansett' and crew. All well," Mr. Morley shouted: "Row straight for the light," the "Gansett's" crew shouted their delight; and in a few moments, with a strong pull on the oars, Faith and Mark sent the little boat well up on the sandy beach, where Mr. and Mrs. Morley, Hallie, and the excited "Jimpsey" were waiting to welcome them.

The sudden tempest at about the time they were expected home had greatly alarmed the Morleys, who, as the hours passed, feared the "Gansett" must have been overturned or swept out to sea.

"It seems as if you children encounter danger wherever you go," Mrs. Morley said, as Mark and Faith added their story to Ellen's hurried tale.

"But we always come safely home, don't we, Aunt Cynthia?" Faith reminded her.

CHAPTER XVII

MISS POLLY LAWTON

As the autumn of 1778 advanced it again became possible for the Morleys to see their Newport friends; and Faith and Ellen, wearing their new gowns, made from the dresses taken from the trunks, with jackets of blue broadcloth, and becoming round caps of the same material, started off one morning soon after their encounter with the British frigate for a long promised visit to Wealthy Richards.

The October morning was clear and sunny, but there was a sharpness in the air that told of the approaching winter. The maples were showing their crimson leaves, and wayside grasses were turning yellow. As the girls walked briskly along over the rough road they stopped now and then to gather stalks of goldenrod, the purple flowers of wild geraniums, and the delicate blooms of Queen Anne's lace that grew along the borders of the highway; so that by the time they entered the town they were both carrying large bunches of the autumn wild flowers.

"Wealthy's mother will like these," Ellen confidently asserted as they approached their friend's house.

"I guess Wealthy will be surprised to see our nice

187

clothes," said Faith, with an admiring glance at Ellen's braided jacket.

But Ellen's thoughts were centered on noticing how many houses bad been destroyed since her last visit; and that trees that had shaded the pleasant streets had been cut down to furnish firewood for the British soldiers. Save for British boats the wharves were deserted; and the beautiful town that for many years had been one of the most important seaports of the American colonies, noted not only for its beautiful location and its fine mansions, but for being the residence of men of great achievements, among them Gilbert Stuart, the painter, Peter Harrison, the architect of Redwood Library, and others of equal importance, was now nearly in ruins; and when the British finally departed, in 1789, it was but a shadow of its former self.

The girls, recalling the shops where Mrs. Morley used to take them to purchase muslins for their summer gowns, or candied fruits brought by ships that so constantly arrived from far ports, now looked wonderingly about the half ruined town.

"There's Wealthy's house," Faith exclaimed, as if she had feared that too might have vanished; and they quickened their pace and were soon at the door, where their knock was promptly answered by Wealthy herself, who danced about exclaiming:

"Oh! I've been looking for you every day this week.

And you have new dresses! I don't believe any other girls in Newport have such pretty gowns," and as Ellen held out the bunches of wild flowers saying they were for Mrs. Richards, the excited Wealthy declared that Faith and Ellen always thought of lovely things for everybody; and hurried them along the hallway to her mother's sitting-room where they received a warm welcome.

"Now come up to my room, girls, and take off your things," she said, after her mother had told them that luncheon would soon be ready; and, talking of the many events that had happened since their last meeting, Wealthy led the way up the broad staircase to a sunny room from whose windows they could see the fine Redwood Library, and look down on the red-coated soldiers who were loitering nearby.

"I guess they are going to stay forever," said Faith, "the British, I mean," she added in response to Wealthy's questioning glance.

"No, they are not," Wealthy declared. "Even if that French fleet didn't drive them away there'll be more French ships come; or else General Washington will."

"Look, girls," called Faith, who had again turned to the window; "isn't that Mistress Polly Lawton?"

"Yes, indeed it is," agreed Wealthy, as the three girls gazed down with admiring approval at the lovely Quakeress, whose father was one of Newport's loyal citizens.

"Oh, I would like to look just like her," said Ellen, as the object of their admiring glances disappeared at a turn of the street.

Ellen was not the only Newport girl who wished she might possess the notable grace and beauty of the sedate and serious young Quakeress, who within the coming year was to receive the admiring homage of a group of distinguished Frenchmen who arrived in the town.

"Mary made me promise to bring you to her house," said Wealthy, as they finished the simple luncheon; and the little group, in the best of spirits, set forth for the Clement house. As they walked along Faith described their adventurous cruise to the island.

"All sorts of things happen to you and Ellen," said Wealthy. "Just think, Faith! When General Prescott was here you met him one day on the road, and—"

"And she saw him carried off from the Overing house, the night Major Barton took him prisoner," interrupted Ellen. "You never knew about that, did you, Wealthy?" and Ellen eagerly recited the story of her cousin's encounter with the Americans in the ravine as they were hurrying Prescott to the shore.

Wealthy listened in amazement. "There! Didn't I say things were always happening to you?" she responded. "I wouldn't wonder if when General Washington comes to Newport Faith would be the first one to speak to him."

"I have a present for him, anyway," Faith smilingly

announced. "I made a box out of that piece of wood from the Liberty Tree, the piece General Prescott spoke to me about; and Ellen made a thimble-box for Lady Washington. If he ever does come to Newport we'll give them to him."

"He's sure to come," Wealthy confidently asserted. "If he doesn't, Faith, you can send him your presents."

"No, if he doesn't come I'll keep my box," Faith soberly replied.

"We'll be grown up by the time he gets here, if he doesn't hurry. We'll be fourteen next year," said Ellen, as they went up the path to the Clement house.

As Mary opened the door for them it was evident that she was not only pleased to see them but that she was pleasantly excited over some bit of good news.

"It's lovely you have come just now," she declared. "Who do you think is here? Mistress Polly Lawton! She is in the sitting-room with mother!" And before the girls could make any response they were being ushered into the room, from whose windows, now over a year ago, they had watched the British soldiers cut down the Liberty Tree.

As Mrs. Clement welcomed them and introduced them to the young Quakeress the girls curtsied, all a little abashed by this unexpected encounter. But Mistress Lawton's radiant smile and friendly greeting at once restored their composure; and Faith, seated beside her, listened admiringly to the pleasant voice as Miss Polly gave them news of D'Estaing, who had lingered long in Boston, where he was handsomely entertained by John Hancock.

"D'Estaing's fleet is sailing for the West Indies; we will not see them here again; but without doubt Lafayette will persuade the French government to send other ships and troops to our aid," she hopefully decried, smiling at Faith, as if confident that no one could question such a statement.

Ellen, seated near a window, soon became uncomfortably aware that the afternoon was drawing to a close; and that, if they were to reach home before sunset, she and Faith should be on their way; so when Miss Lawton rose to take her departure Ellen at once declared that they too must go; and, promising Mary and Wealthy to come again before winter weather made the long walk to Newport too difficult, they proudly accompanied their new acquaintance along the street toward the Lawton house.

As they walked along the cousins admiringly noticed their companion's gown of soft grey wool, with its long cape of the same material, her bonnet of grey silk, and the mitts that covered her hands; and in response to her friendly inquiries they found themselves telling her the story of "Jimpsey"; and of pushing the big boulder into the boat of the raiding party that had endeavored to land at their ledge.

"Why, you girls deserve almost as much credit as the

men who captured General Prescott. But 'tis indeed a pity this dreadful conflict must go on," Miss Polly soberly responded.

"I'd well like to see thy little spaniel. Perhaps thee will bring him when thee comes to see me," she added, as they reached the entrance to the Lawton house, and she bade her new friends good-bye.

The cousins had so much to talk of as they walked briskly along the highway that they paid little attention to the gathering twilight.

"'Tis good fortune we wore our new gowns," said Ellen, "but do you not wish we could have bonnets and mitts like Mistress Lawton's, Faith? And do you think we could take 'Jimpsey' to see her? Oh, just as soon as I am really grown up I mean to have dresses just like hers. I wish we had told her about our cave. Maybe next summer we can ask her to visit us, and show her just where we pushed the boulder off the ledge."

Faith soberly agreed; but her thoughts were a little troubled as she recalled how many secrets they had confided to their new friend.

"Ellen, maybe we talked too much about ourselves. You know, Aunt Cynthia tells us often that 'tis not good manners to talk of our own affairs to strangers."

"Why, 'Zano'!" and Ellen came to a sudden halt and gazed at her cousin in amazement.

"Miss Polly Lawton isn't a 'stranger.' She was born

and grew up here, just as we did. And she asked us to come and see her. I mean to ask Mother to let us go next week, and to take 'Jimpsey.'"

Before Faith could reply "Jimpsey's" joyous bark reached their ears as the spaniel came bounding toward them, with Mark closely behind him.

A few days after this Newport visit, on October 28th, 1778, there came so glorious a local naval exploit that even Faith and Ellen could talk of little else, and the prospective joy of the visit to Mistress Polly Lawton was for a time forgotten, as they listened to Mr. Morley telling of Major Silas Talbot's capture of the Pigot galley, by which the east passage of Narragansett Bay was cleared from control of the British.

The Pigot galley was a stout brig, from which the upper deck had been removed, and guns mounted on the lower deck. Besides these, the galley was strongly protected all around by a high bordering net.

Major Talbot, with the approval of General Sullivan, planned to attack this galley by night, and fitted out the coasting sloop, the *Hawk*, with sixty men and two three-pounders. Favored by a strong wind he sent the sloop at full speed against the galley and Talbot and his men leaped on board before the surprised crew could make but little resistance; only their young commander, Lieutenant Dunlop, made a brave effort against them. But he was quickly overpowered, and the triumphant Americans were in possession of the galley.

As Ellen's birthday approached she announced that she meant to celebrate it by going to visit Mistress Lawton.

"Faith and I promised her we would, Mother," she pleaded; and Mrs. Morley, bidding the girls to remember that Miss Polly was a young lady and might not be interested in the work and games which amused two young girls, gave her permission; and, recalling Miss Polly's wish to see the adventurous "Jimpsey," it was decided that the spaniel should accompany them.

"Jimpsey" was now a well trained and well behaved dog, and there was little chance that he would ever again encounter his former owner; and the two cousins eagerly looked forward to introducing him to the young Quakeress.

The March day proved unexpectedly warm, and Faith and Ellen were well pleased to wear their gowns of checked silk, with the short jackets made from the cape of blue broadcloth and their round hats of the same material; and, with "Jimpsey" trotting soberly at their heels, they set off early in the afternoon.

As they drew near the Lawton house Ellen began to fear that, after all, it was a mistake to have brought the spaniel.

"Maybe we had best leave him outside, 'Zano.' Some folks don't like dogs," she said.

"Miss Polly will," Faith confidently responded, as she clanged the heavy brass knocker on the Lawton door, which was instantly opened by a smiling negro woman.

"Will you please tell Mistress Polly Lawton that Ellen Morley and Faith Underwood and their dog 'Jimpsey,' have come to see her," said Faith.

"Step in, young ladies; and the nice dog, too," said the approving servant.

"It's just as if she were expecting us," thought Faith, as, before they were really inside the door, Miss Polly came hurrying down the stairway smiling a welcome.

"I have expected thee long before this," she declared, "and is this the English dog?" and her white hand smoothed the spaniel's silky head as she led her young visitors into a long room where a fire blazed in a wide brick fireplace.

"If you please, Miss Polly, 'Jimpsey' is an American dog now," ventured Faith.

"To be sure he is," laughed the young lady, drawing them toward a wide wooden settle near the windows, where "Jimpsey" promptly established himself as near Miss Polly's grey silk skirts as possible. And even when the smiling colored maid brought in a tray with cups of creamy cocoa and plates of sweet biscuit, he did not move until Miss Polly, declaring that "Jimpsey" had the best of good manners, fed him one of the biscuits.

"It was all just as if we were grown up, wasn't it, Faith?" declared the delighted Ellen, as remembering her mother's warning not to make too long a stay, the girls bade their admired hostess good-bye and started for home.

"Just exactly, 'Verra.' And I know what I'm going to do. I am going to give Miss Polly that box I made for General Washington," Faith soberly announced.

"Oh, Faith Underwood!" and Ellen stared at her cousin as if Faith had declared disloyalty to the American fight for its liberties.

"I am, 'Verra,'" her cousin firmly asserted.

"Well, then, I shall give her the thimble-box. We had a beautiful visit, didn't we, Faith? And Miss Polly never guessed it was my birthday party," responded the good-natured Ellen; and happily planning another visit when they would carry their gifts to the lovely young Quakeress, the two girls walked leisurely along toward home.

CHAPTER XVIII

THE BRITISH LEAVE NEWPORT

Faith and Ellen made various plans as to the best way of presenting their gifts to their new friend; and at last, happily recalling Miss Polly's interest in the cave, they decided that as soon as the weather grew warm they would invite her to be their guest, and introduce her to "Verrazano."

"And you must tell her about that deserter, Faith," said Ellen, who often felt that her cousin received little credit for the courage she had undoubtedly shown in that encounter.

Although the spring of 1779 was not an encouraging time for the American cause, the people of Newport began to feel confident that the time was near when the British, who had been in control of the town since December 1776, would soon take their departure. They knew that earlier in the year Lafayette had sailed from Boston for France, in the *Alliance*, on a mission to bring aid for General Washington; and there was good news of the success of American ships in their encounters with the English.

In April, Hopkins with a squadron of three vessels sailed from Boston and overtook a fleet of English storeships which General Clinton had sent from New York to Georgia, capturing eight out of the ten vessels; and as the spring advanced Mark Morley kept a sharp outlook over Newport harbor hoping to again see French ships in the offing.

Early in June, Faith and Ellen again stood at the door of the Lawton house; but this tine they made the briefest of visits, as they had come only to ask Mistress Polly if she would give them the pleasure of her company one afternoon of the following week.

"We are asking Mary Clement, and Letty Stevens and Wealthy Richards, and Hallie will make us a chowder," Faith carefully explained, a little fearful lest the lovely young Quakeress who, despite the plainness of her simple gowns, seemed to belong in a world of which they had little knowledge, would think their plan for her entertainment absurd.

"Of course I will come. And will Tuesday be a good day for thee to have me? And will thee bid thy friends to call for me, that we may walk out together?" she responded with such evident pleasure that the cousins smiled at each other.

Tuesday was promptly declared to be just the right day; and Mary, Letty and Wealthy were bidden to call for Miss Polly and bring her safely to the Morley farm.

"Now if it will only be pleasant Tuesday, 'Verra,' it will be the best party we ever had," said Faith, as they happily started for home.

"Let's have the puppets in the cave, 'Zano.' Mark can fix a screen, and have the 'Victory.' I know Mistress Lawton would like it," suggested Ellen.

"That will be splendid. And, Ellen, can't we have the Fairy Queen give her the boxes! Oh! We must give them to her that way," responded Faith, her cheeks flushing with excitement at what seemed to her a perfect way of bestowing their gifts; and as Ellen eagerly agreed they at once began discussing just the right way in which the Fairy should offer the boxes.

"There's lots of wild roses now. We can make the cave lovely," said Ellen; and on the following Monday the two girls worked happily at covering the rough walls of "Verrazano" with branches of fragrant blossoms. The screen, behind which Mark was to manage the puppet show, was cleverly contrived by a frame of poles and an old fish net through which they could weave vines and blossoms; and when early Tuesday morning the girls hurried up the ledge and gazed into the cave they exclaimed in delighted satisfaction.

"It's lovely! It's just where a fairy would make gifts," declared Ellen.

At an early hour of the afternoon Faith discovered their friends coming up the lane and she and Ellen hastened down the slope to welcome them.

Miss Polly, in her gown of grey linen with its wide white collar, and wearing a neat bonnet of shirred muslin, seemed more beautiful than ever to the admiring girls, and when Mary Clement whispered: "How did you know this was Miss Polly's birthday?" Faith was sure that this would be the happiest of days.

And apparently Miss Polly agreed with her; she declared the cave "fairylike," much to Ellen's satisfaction, and exclaimed admiringly over the puppets that Mark managed with great success. And when the Fairy Queen appeared and Mark softened his voice to repeat the lines Faith had taught him:

> "Made of wood from our Liberty Tree
> These two boxes I give to thee.
> One box for a thimble and one for a treasure
> To hold more love than a box can measure,"

and as Faith and Ellen curtsied before her, holding out their gifts, the young Quakeress looked about her in evident surprise, and said:

"Why, 'tis surely fairyland; and thy gifts are beautiful. I shall ever value them," and eagerly questioned the two cousins about the wood of which the boxes were made, and praised their skilful work.

It was a day long to be remembered by the little group. Miss Polly quite approved of the fine name the girls had given the cave; she gazed down at the ledge from which the girls had pushed the boulder into the raiders' boat, and listened with wondering approval to Faith's story of discovering the deserter and of aiding his escape.

"Thee will surely see him again," she said. "I doubt not that he will some day come to thank thee. The British will not be here much longer. General Gates has now been appointed to succeed General Sullivan in command of the American forces of Rhode Island; and our good friend Lafayette will bring us aid," and with these hopeful words she bade them good-bye, leaving the two cousins so happily excited over the success of their well planned entertainment that Mark declared they had lost their wits.

The summer days of 1779 proved a time of many hopeful rumors; and when in October the British at last departed from Newport Faith and her cousins stood on the ledge above the little cove and joyfully watched the ships sail out of the harbor they had so long controlled.

"If only the French ships had driven them out," said Faith. For the failure of D'Estaing's expedition in 1778 had been a deep disappointment.

And now Newport was to bear the disasters the enemy had left behind them. Three hundred houses had been destroyed, shade trees and orchards cut down, and public buildings sadly damaged. Nevertheless the inhabitants were joyful indeed over their freedom from British control. And when in July 1780, Admiral Chevalier de Ternay convoying fifty-five hundred French troops, commanded by Lieutenant-General Comte de Rochambeau, in six ships, came to anchor off Brenton's Point in Newport harbor there was no enemy to give them battle.

Again Faith and her cousins saw the "lilies of France" waving at the mastheads of Admiral de Ternay's still-masted ships; and her Newport friends told her that Rochambeau had taken up his quarters in the stately William Vernon house.

For a year to come the brilliant and distinguished group of French officers added grace to Newport's social life; and Ellen and Faith, visiting Miss Polly Lawton, more than once encountered the Chevalier de Chastellux, whose quiet tastes made him a sincere admirer of the lovely young Quakeress.

The two cousins often talked of the adventurous days, now so happily past, and wondered as to the fate of the deserter. But Miss Polly's prediction came true; for, shortly after the arrival of the French fleet, Hugh Ramsay appeared at the Morley farm.

He had found friends in Tiverton, and declared that he meant to make that his future home. And, greatly to Mark's delight, he brought back the treasured flint and steel that Faith had given him.

"But for the courage and kindness of this little maid I could never have made my escape," he said, smiling at Faith, "and I shall always remember that she was my first friend in America."

It was in March 1781, that Miss Polly invited the two cousins to be her guests for the day of General Washington's arrival in Newport.

"'Tis to be the greatest day Newport has ever seen. The French plan to show him every honor, and thee must not fail to see his arrival," she said; and Faith and Ellen eagerly looked forward to the great event, and were at the Lawton house in time to hear the thunder of the guns of the French fleet as they boomed out their salute of welcome.

Standing on the porch of the Lawton house, where they found Mary, Letty and Wealthy, they watched the French soldiers as they formed a double line from Long Wharf to the State House; and saw Rochambeau, hat in hand, escort Washington to his headquarters in the Vernon house.

The two cousins were to be Miss Polly's guests for the night, that they might see the illumination of the town in honor of the great general. And when Miss Polly suggested that she would well like to give the box made of the wood of the Liberty Tree to General Washington, and to tell him its story, that it had been made by a little maid of Newport, Faith felt that no greater delight would ever come to her, and gladly approved the suggestion.

Washington's departure from Newport was speedily followed by that of Rochambeau's army; and on October 14th, 1781, the British forces under Cornwallis surrendered at Yorktown, Virginia, and the great conflict between England and the American colonies was at an end.

"Our play of 'Victory' has come true, hasn't it, Faith!" said Ellen, when the news reached Newport that Cornwallis had surrendered. "Don't you remember the verse? It ended:

'And Newport peace and joy shall know.'"

Faith nodded smilingly.

"Well, we have 'Jimpsey' to remind us that the British were here," she responded.

"And General Washington has the box made of the wood of the Liberty Tree; and Miss Polly told him about Hugh Ramsay, and about our pushing the boulder into the raiders' boat, and about the night when Major Barton captured Prescott. Oh, 'Zano,' do you know what he said?" Ellen eagerly questioned.

"Of course I do, 'Verra,' and you remember it just as well as I do," Faith laughingly replied. "He said we had courage and sense."

"Yes, and he said it was to be expected that a little maid of Newport would be brave," interrupted Ellen, and the two cousins smiled happily at each other as they again recalled the adventures of the days when the ships of England menaced the town of Newport.

THE END